MASQUERADE

CANTERWOOD CREST

MASQUERADE

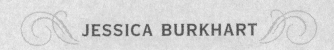 JESSICA BURKHART

ALADDIN M!X

New York London Toronto Sydney New Delhi

This book is a work of fiction. Any references to historical events, real people, or real locales are used fictitiously. Other names, characters, places, and incidents are the product of the author's imagination, and any resemblance to actual events or locales or persons, living or dead, is entirely coincidental.

ALADDIN M!X

Simon & Schuster Children's Publishing Division

1230 Avenue of the Americas, New York, NY 10020

First Aladdin M!X edition September 2012

Copyright © 2012 by Jessica Burkhart

All rights reserved, including the right of reproduction

in whole or in part in any form.

ALADDIN is a trademark of Simon & Schuster, Inc., and related logo

is a registered trademark of Simon & Schuster, Inc.

ALADDIN M!X and related logo are registered trademarks

of Simon & Schuster, Inc.

For information about special discounts for bulk purchases,

please contact Simon & Schuster Special Sales

at 1-866-506-1949 or business@simonandschuster.com.

The Simon & Schuster Speakers Bureau can bring authors to your live event.

For more information or to book an event contact

the Simon & Schuster Speakers Bureau at 1-866-248-3049

or visit our website at www.simonspeakers.com.

Designed by Jessica Handelman

The text of this book was set in Venetian 301 BT.

Manufactured in the United States of America 0812 OFF

2 4 6 8 10 9 7 5 3 1

Library of Congress Control Number 2012942887

ISBN 978-1-4424-3655-8

ISBN 978-1-4424-3656-5 (eBook)

To those on Team Canterwood
who share Lauren's Halloween birthday!

ACKNOWLEDGMENTS

Giant plastic pumpkins filled with candy to the trick-or-treaters at Simon & Schuster: Fiona Simpson, Aly Heller, Bethany Buck, Mara Anastas, Jessica Handelman, Nicole Russo, Courtney Sanks, Carolyn Swerdloff, Russell Gordon, Karin Paprocki, Valerie Shea for copyediting, Craig Adams, and Katherine Devendorf.

Team Canterwood, think of Lauren's party as one thrown in your honor! Each and every one of you deserves a year's supply of candy for supporting the series. ☺

Balloons to Monica Stevenson and the models for a party-perfect cover.

Kate Angelella, it was only fitting that Lauren's fave holiday be yours, too. Each note and comment took my ideas and made them right. LT's party wouldn't be nearly as glam without the distinctive KA touch. A true editor at heart is one who can't help but be excited about a book's progress and offer suggestions from a hospital bed. ♥

Lauren Barnholdt, thank you for writing with me during #1k1hr! Bri Ahearn, you cheered me on from outline to now. Ross Angelella, sorry there aren't any zombies at Lauren's party. ;)

MASQUERADE

MEET MY NEW BFF—
JUDGE NELSON!

A SHINY, SILKY BLUE RIBBON GLEAMED FROM Whisper's bridle. The judge who'd pinned it there extended her hand to me. I shifted Whisper's reins to one hand and read the judge's name badge. MS. NELSON. I leaned down and shook her hand. This did *not* feel real.

"Congratulations, Miss Towers," Ms. Nelson said, smiling. The brunette in a navy suit had appeared so intimidating when I'd ridden for her a short while ago. But now, I kind of wanted to crown her as my new BFF! She *had* given me a blue ribbon, after all.

"Thank you, Ms. Nelson," I said.

My head felt as though it was going to float away from my body and into the cloudless sky. I truly hadn't focused on a ribbon during my first class with Whisper. My goal had been to do our best. Cliché, but true.

That was New Lauren—a competitor who thought of riding well first and placing later. Old Lauren, pre-Canterwood Lauren, would have accepted the ribbon, added it to her collection, and started focusing on the next show. The next chance to win.

But today . . .

My first show since my almost career-ending accident at Red Oak Horse Trials.

My first competition as a Canterwood Crest Academy student.

My first time riding in front of judges on *my* own horse.

Whisper and I had tried our hardest and had given everything we had in the arena—that had been enough for me to be happy. The win was icing on a *très* yummy carrot I planned to give Whisper later. A snort from a horse around me pulled me out of my thoughts.

"Blue looks good on you guys," Lexa Reed said. Next to me, she had a red ribbon on Honor's bridle. Lexa, a close friend, was also on Canterwood's intermediate riding team with her strawberry roan mare.

"Thanks, Lex," I said. "And congrats! We're so celebrating tonight!"

"Um, *yeah*." Lexa smiled, doing a quick dance in the saddle. She glanced around as if looking to see if anyone saw. I tried to hold back a giggle, but it escaped from my lips. Lexa couldn't stop herself from dancing, and I felt as if I'd had a little too much green tea.

The judges motioned for us to exit the arena. Lexa and I followed a girl on a black gelding who'd come in third. Honor and Whisper had each set a hoof on the grass outside the arena when Lexa and I couldn't hold it in for another second.

"Number one and two!" Lexa said. "So awesome!" Her smile was bright against her mocha-colored skin. A quick surge of relief pumped through me. My mind had shifted back to Old Lauren's for a moment, and I'd worried that Lexa would be jealous of my win or mad that I'd beaten her. But that wasn't Lexa. She was a true friend, and Lex was genuinely happy about our placements.

"We showed everyone how Canterwood riders compete," I added. "To win!"

"Yeah, we did." Lexa's happiness radiated to Honor, and the mare picked up on it. Her neck arched and she half pranced. Whisper, watching Honor, copied her. Her delicate gray head went high into the air as she lifted each hoof a little higher than necessary.

We walked the horses away from the arena and back to a quiet spot under a shady tree. The campus was swarming with riders from four area schools, but Lexa and I had been lucky enough to stake out a place to relax before our next class. Khloe, my other BFF and roomie, had been cheering us on from here, but she was gone.

"Did Khloe have a class?" I asked.

"Don't think so. She'll prob be right back. Or maybe she's off practicing, oh, a mean girl, or a competitive girl, or some other persona she might need in her acting repertoire."

Giggling, we dismounted and high-fived.

"Having an actor for a BFF keeps things interesting," I said.

Lexa nodded. "Life in Khloe Kinsella's circle is *never* boring."

We turned our attention to the horses. I petted Whisper's neck. "You were the superstar, girl. I want to hug you like crazy, but we have trail class left. I don't want to mess up your braids or get covered in Whisper hair and lose points for appearance."

Lexa kissed Honor's muzzle. The beautiful strawberry roan mare squeezed her eyes shut, clearly enjoying the affection.

We loosened the horses' girths and gave them tiny sips of water from a shared yellow bucket. Mike and Doug, two of the stable grooms, were doling out water buckets to the competing horses.

Whisper's gray coat was dry under her saddle pad, and she didn't show any signs of nerves from all of the action. She also didn't exhibit symptoms of fatigue—either from stress or our class.

"I couldn't love you more," I told Whisper. "You treated that class like any old lesson. Wait till we're done for the day."

Whisper flicked an ear in my direction and lowered her trimmed, velvety muzzle into my hand. I kissed it and scratched under her forelock.

"Laur! Lex!"

We looked up and a blonde bounced up to us, leading a bay mare.

"Ahhh! Congratulations again!" Khloe said. She ground tied Ever, who reached out her muzzle to say hello to Honor and Whisper. "I'm so glad that I got to watch you both get your ribbons."

"Thanks, KK," I said. "It feels like . . . I don't even know!"

"Awww," Khloe said, winking at Lexa. "Our LT is in shock. Should we pour cold water on her?"

"Let's *not* pour cold water on her," I said, playing along. "Lauren would have to retaliate in the middle of the night. Something involving glitter and glue, perhaps."

Lexa took off her helmet, full-out laughing. "I kind of want this to happen so I can see whatever glitter idea you have!" She ran a hand over her curly black hair. It was in a chic low bun—not loose and down like Lex usually wore it. Natural reddish highlights made her dark skin look even prettier, and a single coat of mascara made her deep brown eyes look bigger.

Khloe shot Lex a pretend *I'm going to hurt you* look. "I'd like to remain glitter *and* glue free, thank you very much. So I'll skip the cold water."

Khloe's brown eyes had a playful look when they landed on me. She certainly didn't look like she'd been up since four this morning. Her tan, freckle-free skin was sans makeup except for clear gloss. We'd both woken instantly when the alarms had gone off hours ago. Adrenaline during show day wasn't something I could sleep through. If only it was that easy to wake up on school mornings!

"Truce?" I asked, tilting my head.

"Truce." Khloe shook my hand, looking serious.

I unsnapped my black velvet-covered helmet and clipped it to Whisper's saddle.

"Here comes someone for Lauren," Lexa said in a sing-song voice.

"What? Who?"

I turned. *He* headed our way. Drew Adams. An insta-smile came to my face. Drew and his blood bay gelding, Polo, hadn't competed in the intermediate dressage class. When I'd entered the ring, I wished Drew had been able to see my ride. See me in my element. But when my name had been called for a ribbon, I'd spotted Drew cheering for me. He'd been in the stands the whole time.

"Hey," he said, smiling at all of us before his gaze settled on me.

"Hi," I said.

"Awesome ride, Lauren." Drew stretched a hand to rub Whisper's neck. "You and Whisper deserved first."

I felt my fair cheeks start to flush. I tried to think of something—anything else but the cute guy standing in front of me—but my mind blanked.

"Thank you," I said. "I came out of the arena feeling like we'd done our best, but I had serious competition. Like Lexa." I tipped my head in my friend's direction.

"Sorry, Lex," Drew said. "I saw your ride too. It's too bad there couldn't have been a tie. Honor executed those turns beautifully."

Lexa waved her hand. "Second place is what we deserve. Lauren and Whisper blew us away. I'm so happy for her! Plus, it's going to make Honor and me raise our game."

Lexa was such a great friend. Gracious, positive, but still competitive. She was the best kind of teammate I could hope for—someone who was there for her fellow teammates even when it came down to individual ribbons.

"How does it feel?" Drew asked. He stepped closer and patted Whisper's shoulder. His sea-blue eyes were soft. I could stare into them forever. They stood out against his black hair and looked like gemstones against his pale skin.

He wasn't asking how it felt to win. "I feel like I can finally close the door on Red Oak," I said. "I needed this—a show—to be able to move a thousand percent past what happened."

Drew smiled, and I couldn't help but do the same. "That's great. I'm happy for you."

"How're you doing?" I asked. "You had cross-country, right?"

Drew shook his head. "Yeah, but we're talking about *you*. About your win."

"Drew! I asked you! How'd it go? Tell me!" I lightly pushed his arm.

"Okay, okay!" He laughed, holding up a hand in a

conceding gesture. He reached under his helmet, which was hanging on Polo's saddle. There was a flash of blue, and he produced a winning ribbon.

"Omigod! Congratulations!" I said, shaking my head. "I wish I could have seen your ride. Why didn't you tell me?"

"Yeah," Lexa chimed in. "Drew, that's great."

"I really didn't want to take away from your moment," Drew said. "I was going to tell you guys later."

It was official—Drew was the sweetest guy e-v-e-r.

"You wouldn't have 'taken away from' my moment," I said.

"She's Lauren Towers," Khloe said. She waved her hand at me in a look-at-this-girl gesture. "Canterwood Crest Academy student and winner of her first class of the season."

Her words took a second to sink in. I glanced around at each of my friends.

Nothing was going to take away my new title. And I wasn't talking about my win.

2

UNSTOPPABLE FORCE

KHLOE'S DRESSAGE CLASS WAS UP NEXT. The schedule worked out so that Lexa and I could watch Khlo's class before we had trail riding. Lex and I stood next to Honor and Wisp on the sidelines of the dressage arena. A cross-country class had just started, and off in the distance, I saw a group of riders waiting for their turn to begin.

"I'm so excited to watch KK," I said to Lexa. "I feel bad that we're not there for Cole, though."

"I know. I wish he'd been in our dressage class, but there were too many entrants."

"It wasn't awful that we didn't have to compete against him, too. It was hard enough to go up against you!"

Lexa leaned into Honor, and the mare closed her eyes.

"I hate that part too. I wish we didn't have to compete against each other."

"Any news on Clare?" I asked.

"Oh! We passed each other, and she said she'd snagged fourth in her show-jumping class."

"That's awesome. She has a pleasure class left, right?" I couldn't keep everyone's schedules straight.

"I think it's happening now. Or maybe the next round."

"I'm excited to watch Khloe. I'm sure I'm going to pick up a bunch of tips."

She nodded. "Me too. I always learn something from watching her ride."

Khloe, looking relaxed as she chatted with a girl that I didn't know, waited with a group of riders while a guy on a compact Morgan worked through his test.

"It's nice to watch someone else before we compete again."

"I can't wait to catch up with everyone once today's over and see where we all placed," Lexa said. "I have a feeling, though, that Canterwood is kicking butt."

"For sure! We're—"

"Khloe Kinsella, please enter the arena," a man's voice crackled on a microphone. "Again, Khloe Kinsella of Canterwood Crest Academy, please enter the arena for advanced dressage."

"Good luck, Khlo," I whispered.

"Go, Khloe," Lexa said, her voice soft.

Ever and Khloe paused at the arena's entrance and started forward at a working trot. They looked like they belonged at the Rolex Kentucky. Khloe had added a black jacket to her outfit, and she appeared professional from helmet to shiny boots.

Ever, her Hanoverian mare, took smooth steps to the arena's center. The tall bay's coat shone from the sunlight, and her button braids were tight and perfect. The only white spot on Ever's body, a white star on her forehead, looked as if Khloe had just washed it.

Khloe halted Ever at X, dipped her head, and saluted the judges. I caught myself holding my breath. I wanted to yell out "Good luck" to Khloe, but instead I repeated it in my head.

Khloe and Ever proceeded at a working trot to C, where they tracked right and made a flawless twenty-meter circle to B.

"Gorge," Lexa whispered.

"Completely," I said.

With invisible cues from Khloe, Ever sailed through

the test, completing a working canter on both left and right leads, more circles, a medium walk. I lost myself in her ride. I watched the moves she made—squinting to see *everything*. Khloe was one of the best dressage riders I'd ever seen. I was glad that we weren't competing against each other—I wasn't ready to go up against someone like Khloe. A couple of years ago, I would have been. But not now. Khloe and Ever were an unstoppable force—nothing like the riders I'd just seen before them.

The horse and rider were beautifully in sync. It was a rarity to have *that* kind of match. Somehow, the universe had paired Khloe and Ever, and their hard work was clear.

Khloe signaled Ever to move into a free trot down the center. My roomie halted Ever, who stopped perfectly square, and she saluted the judges.

Cheers erupted from the stands. Even competitors from other schools clapped or whistled for Khloe. It had been a ride that deserved recognition from *all* schools.

"Go, Khloe!" Lexa yelled, clapping.

"Yay, Khlo!" I cheered. "Woo!"

Khloe and Ever left the arena, and the clapping didn't stop until one of the judges called the next competitor.

Khloe rode Ever up to Lexa and me, her cheeks pink.

"Um, Khloe Kinsella," I said. "You are a dressage queen. Oh, my God."

"Oh, please," Khloe said. She shook her head, smiling and rolling her eyes. "You're my BFFL and you have to say that. We did our best—that's all that matters."

Lexa took Ever's reins, holding them under her chin, so Khloe could dismount. "Stop, Miss Modesty! That test was, as Laur would say, *très parfait*—and the judges would be crazy not to give you the blue."

Khloe hopped lightly to the ground, smiling her thanks at Lexa as she took Ever's reins. "Well, thank you both, but we'll see how everyone else does." She turned to me. "I've got this weird superstition where I don't watch people after me or listen to their scores."

"I get that," I said. "What about hearing your own score? It's going to be announced in a minute."

Khloe took off her helmet. "Nope. I don't want to know until the end. Then I'll take the score and learn where I was marked up and need to improve. Ever and I did all we could, and *this* round is over." She shrugged. "Nothing I can change about it."

We all had our own show-related rituals. Lexa and I kept Khloe occupied while the rest of the competitors completed their tests. My mind kept slipping in and out of the convo and back to Khloe's ride. She was a Canterwood rider—it was in her blood.

And it showed.

It was my goal that one day, Whisper and I would be a pair like Khloe and Ever. Whisper, eager to learn and trying hard, wasn't as seasoned as Khloe's older mare. It didn't feel like a disadvantage to me, though, because *I* got to train Whisper. We were going to grow together. I hoped to prevent Whisper from learning any bad habits that she could have picked up if she'd been competing with lots of other riders before me. Every rider had a different style, and I wanted Wisp to know only mine.

As for Khloe versus me—that was a little different. I used to ride like that on the A circuit. I had been off the show circuit long enough to have lost my edge—the razor-sharp edge needed to go up against a rider at Khloe's level. A level that I was determined to reach again.

Together, Whisper and I were a new pair. We would both require much more training before we'd be an even match for my roomie and her horse. And that was perfectly fine with me.

I shook myself out of my thoughts, reaching out to stroke Ever's neck. The bay was so sweet.

"Did you see that girl from Saint Agnes?" Khloe asked us.

"The one on the black gelding that's almost big enough to be a draft horse?" Lexa asked, rolling her eyes.

"I didn't—oh, wait! I did see her! She bumped her horse into Whisper during warm-ups," I said.

Khloe shook her head. "That's Peyton. I know somebody who knows somebody at Saint Agnes who said Peyton went to *Europe* for a while to train, and she just got back for the year. She's in this class too."

Lexa groaned, stepping closer to Khloe and me. The three of us were sandwiched close together with our horses beside us. "That means we're going to see her at every single show."

That named sounded so familiar. But neither the girl who'd glared at me nor her horse had registered.

"I'm staying far away from her," I said. "She's a com—"

"And now," the microphone boomed. Someone had turned the volume a little too loud.

Whisper tossed her head and shook her neck. "It's okay," I said. "Easy." I ran a hand down Whisper's neck, feeling her tight muscles shiver.

"Please direct your attention to the dressage arena for results of the advanced dressage class." Ms. Nelson had the microphone now.

"Eeeek! Guys! Ahhh! Nervous! " Khloe said, spitting

out the words. Her face flushed, and she clasped her hands together. "I hate this part!"

"You *won*," Lexa said. "I know it!"

"LEX!" Khloe half yelled. Her voice broke the quiet that surrounded us. Horses *and* riders turned their heads toward the scream. Lexa and I ducked our heads. I eyed Khloe, who had her head up and glanced around, pretending she was looking for the noisy culprit too. My eyes met Lexa's, and I could tell she was giggling on the inside too.

"I was just trying to say," Khloe said in a fast and furious whisper, "that I'm superstitious about other people saying I've won or done a good job before the results are announced."

"Since when?" Lexa whispered back.

"Five minutes ago," Khloe said. She gave Lex a sweet smile, put on her helmet, and mounted.

Lexa shook her head, but didn't say anything as the judges took turns announcing the lower-ranked ribbon holders.

Fourth place—not Khloe.

Third place—not Khloe.

Second place—not Khloe.

"In first, please congratulate . . ."

I bit the inside of my cheek. *Please say Khloe!*

". . . Khloe Kinsella, riding Ever from Canterwood Crest Academy!"

"Yay!" I looked up at a beaming Khloe.

"Told you so!" Lexa said. She grinned, then stuck up a hand for Khloe to high-five.

Khloe trotted Ever away from us and through the arena entrance. She halted the mare next to Peyton, who had claimed second place. I compared Peyton's score to Khloe's—only a point and a half had separated them. Khloe, smiling, didn't seem to notice Peyton's stony stare. Khloe and Ever accepted their blue ribbon. Another win for Canterwood—check!

I cheered for my roomie until my throat was sore and my hands stung from clapping.

3

OUT OF (SHOW) SHAPE

EXCITEMENT HIT ME WHEN I APPROACHED the big arena for my trail class. Before Canterwood, I'd always forced myself to take the toughest classes when anything fun had been offered. Or I'd been too high up on the show circuit for anything like this to be an option for me.

Lexa and Honor had ridden before me and were watching me on the sidelines. Honor had a great round, except she'd gotten scared of the wooden bridge and had tried to refuse crossing. Lexa, like a pro, had gotten Honor over the obstacle after a second try.

Before my class, I'd had time to grab a prepacked lunch that was offered to riders. Cole, Lexa, Clare, Drew, Khloe, and I all had gathered on the bleachers and enjoyed bottles of lemonade, chips, and PB&J sandwiches. Then we'd scattered to our classes.

Now I focused on what was ahead. I walked Whisper up to the gate—the first obstacle. I had to open and close it without dismounting. Angling Whisper with one hand and maneuvering the gate wasn't easy, but Whisper cooperated, and I latched it behind us before starting to the next challenge. Trail class was so fun!

We weaved through six bright orange traffic cones at a trot and Whisper didn't blink. I slowed her to a walk as we approached a red metal mailbox. It was covered with flowers and ivy. I opened it, the metal hinges squeaking. Whisper shuddered, pricking her ears forward. I tightened my legs around her sides and kept her still. I shut the mailbox and we continued. Whisper didn't balk at stepping over cavalletti or trotting over a log.

We approached a section of the arena that was littered with debris. I kept my hands light and guided Whisper around plastic milk jugs, Tide bottles, various soda cans, and a crumpled neon jacket. I let out a tiny breath of relief when we left that part of the arena. The "debris field" had been one of the challenges I'd been worrying about. Once I'd signed up for trail, I'd made a point to introduce Whisper to new and different objects, but I had no way of knowing what we'd find on the course.

We approached the bridge that had spooked Honor. It was a solid wooden bridge that started flat and gradually rose less than a foot into the air and was long enough for a couple of strides.

You've got this, I thought, trying to reach Whisper. Her head rose, and she eyed the bridge. I put pressure on her sides, letting Wisp know we were going over. She started to weave to the left. *Nope. Not going to happen.* I added more pressure with my left leg and pulled slightly on the right rein. Whisper followed my instruction and straightened her body as she stepped up to the bridge.

I kept up Whisper's momentum, not wanting to give her more time to think about what she was doing. She placed a hoof on the plywood, and her metal shoes clunked against the wood. Whisper's ears flicked in every direction, and she wanted to step back onto the arena dirt. I pushed her forward, tapping her hip with my crop. Another hoof was on the bridge, and soon she stood willingly on the bridge—not one attempt to step off. Now that Whisper was on the obstacle, it seemed to make her calmer to see the end of the bridge.

Wisp covered the bridge at a fast walk and snorted

when she stepped onto the dirt. *Good, good girl!* I wanted to pat her neck, but we had a few obstacles left.

Six red-and-white jumping poles were on the ground— three on each side. I circled Whisper, halting with her tail facing the poles. After a smooth stop, I put pressure on the reins and asked Whisper to back up. She tucked her chin and stayed within the poles as we backed through them.

The rest of the course went by fast. Whisper cantered around barrels, jumped a ditch filled with water, and didn't move when I dismounted, picked up a beach-towel-size piece of blue tarp, and rubbed the crinkly, loud material over her body. I opened and closed the gate behind us, again, and applause made me grin.

"Yay, girl! That was *très magnifique!*" I said. "You're so brave. Especially with that scary tarp. I'm so proud of you."

I walked her back to where Lex and Honor waited.

"High five, LT!" Lexa said, holding up her palm. "Awesome job!"

We slapped palms and grinned at each other. "Thanks!" I said. "Our first show of the season is officially over."

Lexa pulled on Honor's reins as the mare reached for a leaf off the tree beside her. "I'm glad. Embarrassing, but I'm actually *tired*. I'm out of show shape."

"I thought it was just me," I said. "We've got to give ourselves a little slack. It's the first competition of the season. We'll get better."

"Hey, guys." Drew, astride Polo, rode up next to me. A yellow ribbon flashed on Polo's bridle.

"Niiice!" I said, gesturing to the ribbon. "What class?"

"Pleasure," Drew said. "We were *this* close to snagging a better position, but I got sloppy with my posture toward the end." He patted Polo's neck. "Totally my fault. Polo did great."

I loved watching Drew interact with his horse. This look came across his face whenever he talked about Polo, and it only intensified when the two were together. Drew wasn't a rider who was all about winning, but he was competitive at the same time. It was one of the things I really liked about him.

"Third's not bad at all," Lexa said. "All the better that you know where you were off and you can pay attention to it next time."

"That's true," Drew said. He smiled at me. Like an almost-make-you-fall-off-your-horse smile. "You finished with trail?"

"We're both done. I think he's the last rider," I said, nodding to a blond guy in the arena.

"Sorry I missed your rides," Drew said. "Cool if I hang out while you get ribbons?"

"Assuming we're getting ribbons without even seeing out rides?" Lexa raised an eyebrow, smiling. "I like it. Positive thinking will make the judges reward LT and me."

The three of us watched as the guy in the arena finished, latching the gate behind him. His horse had refused to maneuver enough for the Regent County Day rider to close the gate while on horseback. Major points off.

No one talked as the judges calculated the scores. Drew shot me a smile, and I managed a slightly wobbly one back. Whisper and I hadn't encountered any big problems during our ride, but I knew there were probably plenty of places I'd messed up and hadn't realized it. I tried to replay every second of the class in my head. *I hope we at least came in fourth,* I thought. *I have to do well—it's my first show for Canterwood.*

For Mr. Conner.

For Whisper.

For me. But don't forget New Lauren. She knows that Mr. Conner isn't counting every ribbon—won or lost—and that's not what Canterwood's about.

"Riders of the intermediate trail class in arena C, please give your attention to the judges as the ribbons are awarded," Mr. Conner said, speaking into a microphone. He handed it off to Judge Nelson.

"Fourth place . . . is Lexa Reed and Honor for Canterwood Crest Academy," Judge Nelson said.

Lexa looked at me, then Drew, with wide eyes. "Whoa! I didn't think we'd place at all because of the bridge mess-up. Good girl!" Lex stroked Honor's shoulder and rode into the arena, stopping in the center. One of the other judges pinned a white ribbon on Honor's bridle and shook Lexa's hand.

Third place went to a girl from Sterling Preparatory.

I started to flick my tongue against the permanent retainer on my bottom teeth.

"Laur," Drew said quietly.

I looked at him, not saying a word.

"Breathe."

I took a gulp of air, wishing I had a cup of steaming vanilla chamomile tea.

"Second place is Lauren Towers and Whisper from Canterwood Crest Academy."

Wait! What?!

Wide-eyed, I looked at Drew, needing him to verify what I'd just heard.

"I *think* you're the only Lauren Towers at our school,"

Drew said, laughing. "You going to get your ribbon?"

"Omigod! I got second! I wasn't sure I'd heard it right—it was so weird! I—"

"Go!" Drew shook his head, laughing harder.

Giggling, I cued Whisper forward. We passed Lex, and she gave me a thumbs-up.

After the first-place winner had been declared and pinned, we rode out of the arena.

"I think we rocked it," Lexa said. "Canterwood showed those schools!"

"Yeah, we did!" I said.

"Lex!"

Clare, waving a blue ribbon in the air, motioned her friend over.

"What was I just saying about us destroying the other schools?" Lexa asked. "See you in a sec."

"Congrats on the win!" I called to Clare.

She grinned. "Thanks, Lauren!"

"And red looks pretty on you, sweet girl," I told Whisper. I leaned a little closer to her. "And now let's go talk to Drew."

He had dismounted and smiled up at me. "Not a bad haul for your first time out in a while," Drew said. "You should be really proud."

I dismounted, glad my blushing cheeks hid behind Whisper.

"Thanks," I said, peeking around Whisper's neck at him. I undid her girth, giving her more room to breathe.

"I knew it was you."

I turned at the unfamiliar voice and looked up into the eyes of the girl on the black horse. I held her gaze for a second—sure I'd seen those eyes before. But I couldn't place her, and I usually had a decent memory about people's names.

"Sorry, but have we met?" I asked. There was *something* about her that I recognized, but I didn't know what it was. Her name had sounded familiar too, when Khloe had said it earlier, but that was all I had.

Drew took a step closer to me, his eyes shifting between the girl and me.

Peyton laughed. "Oh, Lauren. You're smarter than that. Or at least you *were* when you were on the A circuit." She pouted. "I can't believe you don't remember me. Maybe the hair color and my new horse are throwing you off?"

I stared. "No, I don't—"

"Blond hair. Liver chestnut mare. Your *only* competition on the circuit."

No way.

"Peyton. Carter. Omigod. Oh. Um. Wow."

Say more than one-word sentences! I screamed at myself.

"Blond got boring, so I changed my hair. And my horse went lame, so I sold her."

"Oh, no. I'm sorry about your mare. I remember her— she was sweet."

I couldn't remember the horse's name, but I *did* remember that she did whatever Peyton had asked of her. Peyton wasn't the gentlest of riders. I didn't let myself think *how* her mare had gone lame.

Peyton shrugged. "Sweet doesn't win championships." She rubbed the neck of the horse under her. The black horse was fit, tall, and blacker than coal. There wasn't a single patch of white on him.

"He's gorgeous," I said. Maybe If I was polite and could get away fast enough, Peyton wouldn't start anything.

Peyton shot me an *of course he is* smile. "This is Noir. My parents bought him for me when I went to Germany. He medaled in the Olympics last year, and I just had to have him."

"I can't think of a better present to bring home with you from abroad than a horse."

Peyton smiled sweetly. "If you ever go out of the country, maybe you'll have a chance to find out."

I managed a smile. "Hopefully."

"Enough about me," Peyton said, waving her hand. "Going to introduce us, Lauren?" She nodded at Drew.

"Sorry. Peyton, this is Drew Adams. We both ride for Canterwood."

Peyton flashed a pretty smile at Drew. He gave her a quick smile back, but it was strained. It wasn't his I'm-really-happy smile. Dragging her eyes from Drew, Peyton stared at me with a look in her eyes. A look of *trouble*.

"I heard rumors that you, the national dressage champ, had started riding at Canterwood. I didn't believe it. After that horrible accident . . ." Peyton bit her glossy bottom lip. "I was sure you'd never ride again. But here you are!"

"I took some time off," I said, not sure where this was going. Peyton and I had competed against each other several times, but we'd never been friends. She was the girl everyone had stayed away from—*far* away. Peyton trashed-talked every rider, spread the nastiest rumors, and bragged to anyone within earshot that her parents had spent seven figures on her horse. Some of us joked if she made the grooms line her horse's stall with hundred-dollar bills.

"You mean, you're still taking time off, right? You just finished a *trail* class. An *intermediate* trail class."

Drew cleared his throat, shifting. I didn't have to look to know he was mad. He couldn't have been angrier than I was. Peyton wasn't dumb. She knew exactly what she was doing—she was determined to make it look as if I'd had a fall from grace.

"No, I'm not taking time off now," I said, forcing myself not to snap at her. "I'm back to riding. If that's 'time off,' it's news to me."

Peyton blinked her hazel eyes. "So it's true. You're on the *intermediate* team here." She shook her head, not even bothering to hide the smile that curled on her lips. "You can't ride on the A circuit when you're slumming it by doing trail classes. I'm guessing this was the only show that would allow you to participate, anyway."

I froze. I hadn't expected to see Peyton—or anyone—from my past showing days. Today, of all days, I wanted to enjoy every second of the show. Fighting with girls like Peyton was a waste of energy.

"Payson," Drew said, his tone annoyed.

I shot him a look, then gazed back at Peyton. I had *no* clue what Drew was doing! But if he was going to rip Peyton, he definitely had my SOA!

"It's Peyton," she snapped.

"*Peyton*," Drew said. "I don't know why you're wasting

your breath talking to us. Two intermediate riders who are obviously 'slumming it.'"

Oh.

Mon.

Dieu.

If I could freeze time, I'd jump up and down, and then rewind the moment. Again. And again. And again.

Peyton's head jerked back, but she recovered. "Aw, are you her boyfriend? So sweet of you to stand up for Lauren."

I cringed, feeling warm from head to toe. I didn't consider Drew my boyfriend, not yet anyway, and I was *pretty* sure he didn't think of me as his girlfriend. It seemed like things were going that way, but it was too soon for those labels.

"Drew's my teammate, Peyton," I said. "That's all you need to know."

Peyton glanced back and forth between us as if she was trying to decide whether to go or not. Her gelding yanked his head, stamping his back hoof. Peyton tightened the reins.

"Well, it was good to see you doing *something* at least, Lauren," Peyton said. She turned her eyes to Drew. "If you're hanging around Laur to pick up riding tips—you're wasting your time. She's not the girl that I used to compete against anymore."

A vein throbbed in Drew's neck. I'd never seen him like this. He was so angry—I half worried he'd stride up to Noir and knock Peyton off his back.

I didn't need him to stand up for me; I'd done it for myself since I'd started competing. There was something . . . nice, though, about having someone *want* to help.

"You're probably right," Drew said. "Lauren's not the same person you competed against."

Peyton looked at me with a *ha!* face.

"She's better," Drew finished.

The satisfied look on Peyton's face disappeared. Now it was my turn for a *ha!* look.

4

SURPRISE CALLER

Lauren Towers's Blog

2:23 p.m.: First show!

I can't believe I competed in my first show since Red Oak yesterday. I'm so proud of how everyone on my team and Khloe did. Here's our haul:

CH: first and third

LR: second and fourth

CB: first and fourth

DA: first and third

KK: first and second

Moi: first and second

Um, Go Canterwood! At the end of the show, as the host school, Canterwood students had to help riders

from Regent County Day, Saint Agnes Academy, and Sterling Prep if they needed anything.

When Khloe and I got back to our room, the first thing we did was pin our ribbons on our corkboard. Two blue and two red ribbons look *très belle*!

It hadn't taken the other schools long to leave, and once they did, I headed straight to Whisper's stall with treats. I'd stashed a can of vanilla frosting in the pantry at the stable. I took two carrots from the fridge, covering them in the frosting, and took them to Whisper. It was like she'd known what I was doing! She put her head over the stall door and stretched her neck toward me as I walked up to her.

So. Cute. ☺

I fed her the carrots, and she dribbled orange slime onto my arms. I wouldn't have cared if she'd covered me in carrot juice—she deserved the treats for how hard she'd worked. I feel like a neon sign that had been hovering over my head saying SHE HASN'T SHOWN SINCE RED OAK! is gone. That doesn't mean I'm all "Sweet! First show down and I'm ready to enter every competition and up my difficulty."

But it did boost my confidence.

After pinning our ribbons, K and I took turns showering and slipped into lounge clothes. We grabbed sodas, Doritos, and cupcakes from the common room.

Even though we'd gotten up at four, we were both wide awake. We gave each other the play-by-play of each of our classes. Then I told her about the PC run-in, and she nearly D-I-E-D when I told her what D had done.

Our convo went something like this:

Me: *finishes story of how D made P practically gallop her horse away from us*

K: OMIGOD! OMIGOD! OMIGOD! *puts the back of her hand across her forehead and swoons*

Me: That's just who D is. He would have stood up for any of his friends.

K: *snorts* Yeah, puh-lease. Didn't you pay attention to that scene in last week's *Southampton Socialites*? You're Dinah, and D's River. D defended the honor of the girl he hearts. Just like when River punched that guy who told Dinah that he'd spread that awful rumor about her cheating on all of her old boyfriends. Dinah didn't have time to even say a word before POW, River punched the loser.

Me: *shaking my head* Um, D didn't punch anyone. And I'm not sure if he "hearts" me.

K and I went back and forth forever—she made me tell her every detail down to how D had stood. (Something about him leaning one way or the other, according to *Flirt!*, explained his level of protectiveness toward me. Khloe had declared that he was protective, but knew I could take care of myself.) We'd left it with K concluding that D was going to ask me to be his GF any second.

I don't know about that, but I do know *one* thing: I have one birthday wish. I know you're not supposed to say them aloud, but I don't think typing it counts.

I hope D kisses me on my bday. ♥

Posted by Lauren Towers

I closed my laptop lid, the stickers covering the top making me smile. Hello Kitty. Puffy hearts. Sparkly stars. Horses.

Khloe was at Clare's, watching a movie. She'd invited me, but I'd wanted to blog and maybe Skype with Becca, Ana, or Brielle. Khloe had understood and said she'd wanted to talk about my birthday party plans when she got back. Just the thought made me grin. My birthday was also my favorite holiday—Halloween. Khloe had already promised Becca that she was going to plan the best birthday bash ever, and knowing Khloe, I couldn't wait to see what she'd come up with. Plus, it wasn't far away—only three weeks! Three weeks and I'd be *thirteen*. I wondered if turning thirteen would feel different from any other birthday. It had to. Thirteen was a big deal.

Riiing! Riiing!

I got up from my desk chair and hurried to my nightstand.

On my phone's screen, a photo of a smiling blond, tan guy lit up, and TAYLOR FROST blinked at me.

I swiped my BlackBerry off the stand. Taylor's name wasn't exactly one I'd expected to see on my phone. We'd been BBMing a lot, but hadn't talked much since I'd gotten here.

"Hey, Tay," I said.

"Hi, LaurBell," Taylor said.

The way he said my nickname made me smile. Taylor and I had a special relationship. He'd been my boyfriend for five months while I'd been at Yates. I'd had an insta-crush on him the second I'd seen him. Taylor had said hi to me one day, and that had led us to hallway conversations, which turned into lunch dates, then real dates, and soon we'd been BF and GF.

Taylor and I'd bonded over both being athletes—he was a swimmer. His dedication to swimming made it easy for him to understand my commitment to riding. I'd gone to every swim meet I could, and he asked about every lesson at Briar Creek.

"What's up?" I asked, jumping back to the present.

"I'm surprised you're calling today. Did your dad ease up on the 'Sundays are for family time and homework only' rule?"

Taylor blew out a breath. "Hardly. He had to run to the office, shocker, so I had a few minutes to call. He asked if I wanted to come, but I made a very convincing case that I had too much homework."

"I'm glad you called. Really glad."

Taylor didn't like to talk about his father—an investment banker who was trying to turn Taylor into a mini clone of himself.

"I know it's not your favorite topic, but I want to make sure you're okay. We haven't talked about your dad in a long time. How *are* things?"

This was another aspect of my relationship with Taylor that wasn't exactly common. Or, at least, not common with people I knew who broke up. Last summer, when I'd been accepted to Canterwood, Taylor and I had decided, mutually, to break up. We'd both considered a long-distance relationship. Taylor, however, being the mature guy that he is, wanted more for me. He wanted Canterwood to be a completely fresh start for me. In return, I'd wanted the same for him—to start seventh grade with the option to date whomever he wanted. We cared about each other too much to stay together. I was *incredibly* lucky that Taylor and I had been able to gradually transition our relationship from BF/GF to good friends.

"Eh," Taylor said. "A little more intense than when you were here. He's pressuring me to cut back my hours at the pool so I can spend more time shadowing him at work. I was worried for a while that he was going to make me quit the swim team."

"Oh, Tay! I'm so, *so* sorry!" I plopped onto my bed. "I wish you'd told me. I know how much swimming means to you. It's *your* thing, and you must have been so angry and scared at the thought of having to quit."

"I was going to tell you, but you had enough going on. I was able to convince him that swimming was one of the school sports that actually took up the least amount of time. I mean, it's probably not true, but I had to stay on the team."

"Plus," I said, "you have to have a physical activity at Yates. You could always remind your dad that an extra-curricular like swimming will look good on your transcript, especially if you keep swimming in high school."

Tay laughed. I pressed my ear closer to the phone. I'd missed his laugh. When he thought something was really funny and wasn't laughing to be polite, he laughed so hard it shook his entire body.

"We're on the same page," Tay said. "Since seventh grade is *so* close to college, I reminded him about transcripts, and that helped my case."

"Argh! Your dad has to let you be Taylor Frost— seventh grader at Yates—not Taylor Frost prepping for *college* and on his way to becoming vice president of Frost Investments."

"Feel free to write that as an anonymous letter to my dad," Taylor said. He sighed. "Thanks for asking about that, Lauren. It's not the most fun thing to talk about, but talking to you makes me feel better."

I wished I could hug him. "I'm never too busy to talk about *anything*. You're one of my best friends, Tay. Please, please tell me when something's going on, and even if I can't help, at least you can vent."

"You listened. It helps more than you know."

There was silence for a few seconds. Not an awkward what-do-we-talk-about-now quiet. But a comfortable silence.

"So," I said. "Subject change! Thanks for BBMing me about my show yesterday and being so excited."

"Of course I was excited! I wish I could have been there. How did it feel to compete on your own horse?"

"Surreal. Wisp worked so hard, and I couldn't have asked for more. I've always been proud of the horses

I've rode in the past, but I didn't know I could feel *that* level of pride." I smiled, like always when I talked about Whisper. "I'll have to get one of my friends to videotape us working out and send it to you. There's this connection between us that I think is visible." I giggled. "I know that sounds crazy."

"No, it doesn't," Taylor said. "It sounds like you definitely found your horse soul mate. I'd love to see you ride her. Def get me a DVD."

"I want the same from you," I said. "Have one of the guys tape one of your meets. Deal?"

"Deal."

I settled back onto my pillow and talked to Taylor until my phone beeped from a low battery. When I hung up, there were still so many things we had to talk about.

5

KK: PARTY PLANNER
TO THE ★S

THE DOOR OPENED AND A SMILING KHLOE
came into our room. I'd hung up with Taylor moments ago, plugged in my phone, and was finishing a Chatter message.

"Drop everything," Khloe said. "We are going to do some serious, and I mean *serious*, birthday party planning!"

I smiled. "That sounds awesome. I can't wait to see what my official party planner has in mind."

Khloe hummed "Happy Birthday" as she gathered notebooks, magazines, pens, and her iPad.

I reread my Chatter update and pressed update.

LaurBell: Talked 2 @TFrost until my phone battery died. @AnaArtiste & @BrielleisaBeauty, watch out—ur next! ☺

Khloe motioned for me to join her on the floor. "We need lots of room," Khloe said.

I got off my bed and carefully stepped over the piles and lowered myself to the carpet. "You *didn't* start working on this before the show, did you?" I asked. "Because you promised you wouldn't."

Khloe looked around the room, then grabbed an issue of *Flirt!* "On the most sacred magazine of all that holds celeb gossip, beauty tips, and, everything a girl needs to *live*." Khloe placed her hand flat on the magazine. "I'm starting right now. I kept my promise and didn't begin before the show."

Her seriousness over swearing on *Flirt!* made me giggle. "I believe you. You'd never lie while under the oath of that magazine."

Khloe nodded, flipping her fishtail braid over her right shoulder. "Never."

"Show me what you've got," I said.

"I may not have *written* down anything, but I did have a thought. Obvi, tell me if you totes hate it. It's your birthday, and it has to be everything you want. I promised Becca that I'd throw you the coolest party ever."

I smiled, thinking back to when Khloe had hijacked a Skype convo I'd been having with my older sister. Khloe and Becca had acted like BFFs and almost started planning my party on the spot!

"Becs is *plenty* happy that I found such an awesome friend at school," I said. "She knows no matter what you do—it'll be amazing. And so do I."

Khloe lifted her eyes from her notebook. "Thanks, LT. That means a lot."

"Tell me your idea," I said.

Khloe opened a blank notebook, holding a purple Bic above it. "This is your thirteenth birthday. It's one of the most important birthdays ever. Added bonus: Halloween. I know how much you love it, so what if we combine the two? I'm sure you've had spooky birthday parties when you were a kid, but I have something a *little* different in mind for this one."

"*J'adore* Halloween, of course! And yes, I've had parties with peeled grapes as eyeballs, witch's brew punch, pumpkin sugar cookies, and all of my friends came dressed in costumes. One year, I think there were at least five people in Spiderman costumes."

"Oh, my dear Lauren." Khloe hugged her zebra-print notebook to her chest. "That isn't even close to the kind of party you'll be getting."

I grinned, looking at her. October thirty-first needed to hurry!

"What do you think about throwing a masquerade

ball?" Khloe asked. "The girls will be in gorgeous, glam dresses, and the guys will be in collared shirts and pants. Everyone will come with a mask that matches his or her outfit or personality." She paused, watching my face.

My expression told her everything she needed to know. I was breathy and wide-eyed.

"The masks aren't going to be silly or typical Halloween masks either. I want ornate, beaded, jewel-toned, feathery, handheld masks."

Khloe stopped, took a deep breath, and looked at me, waiting for my answer.

"Khloe Kinsella, if you weren't already such a talented actress, I'd say you should become an event planner. I. Love. This. Omigod! I never would have thought of it! It's going to be *so* luxurious and beautiful. It sounds like a Halloween party that celebrities would have on their Manhattan rooftops."

"Yaaay!" Khloe clapped. "I'm so, so happy you love it!"

"Love it times a million. The masquerade theme incorporates Halloween *and* turning thirteen. It's just the grown-up feel that I wanted." I thought for a minute. "The mask is kind of symbolic in a way. I'll be hiding the face of tween Lauren all night until it's time to take off my mask. Then I'm thirteen with nothing to hide behind."

Khloe scribbled away in her notebook as I talked. "We're lucky because October thirty-first happens to fall on a Saturday this year. It'll give us, and by 'us,' I do *not* mean you, lots of extra time to set up and make sure everything's perfect."

"I can help," I said. "You don't have to do this all by yourself. Khlo, you've got a million things going on right now. The play. Riding. School. Zack."

She waved a dismissive hand at me. "Nope. Sorry. You're not helping with setup. Only tell me everything you want and envision. Plus, I'll have Clare, Lex, Jill, and some other people help me set up."

I eyed her. "Okay, but promise you'll ask me for help if you need it."

"Promise. So . . ." Khloe put her iPad on her lap and opened the Internet. "Let's start with what you're thinking about dress-wise, so I can get a feel for the glam scale."

We peered over the iPad as Khloe logged on to Macy's. Khloe clicked "dresses," then "junior party dresses."

"It's silly," I said. "But I've had an idea of the dress I've wanted to wear for my thirteenth birthday since I turned twelve."

Khloe shook her head. "No way is that silly. That just

means we won't stop looking until we find the dress you've imagined. It has to be *the* one. What does it look like?"

"Hit 'all' and then we can see all seventy-two options," I said. "Macy's has to have it."

"While we're looking, I bet Lex, Jill, and Clare would appreciate it if we e-mailed them links to any gorge dresses that could be options for them."

"Good idea."

Khloe took her time scrolling through the dresses on her iPad. She hovered over a tangerine floral appliqué dress. "Lexa," we both said. Khloe clicked on the dress for details. The sleeveless, fully lined tulle dress had small flowers with pearls in the center on the bodice.

Khloe logged into her Gmail account and pasted the link.

Back on Macy's, I pointed to a strapless sequin dress. "That screams you," I said. "It's black, won't take away from your hair or any accessories, and the satin tie bow is adorable."

"I looove it," Khloe said. "Nice find!" She added the dress to the cart.

We found a dress for Clare—a pleated dress with capped sleeves. The skirt had tulle underlay, and the amethyst color would be striking against her hair. Khloe copied the link and added it to the e-mail.

Khloe continued scrolling slowly through the dresses. We were almost at the bottom of the page, and my heart was sinking. We added a link to a pretty coral dress with a lace mesh tier for Jill. Macy's had a *ton* of cute dresses, but none were The Dress. There were other sites, but—

"Stop! There! Click!" I tapped the tablet screen. "That's it! That's my dress!"

Khloe clicked, and new page loaded with a larger image of my dream dress.

"That is *so* beautiful, Lauren! Omigod!" Khloe pulled on my arm.

I didn't take my eyes off the computer screen. The light pink dress had spaghetti straps and was covered in sequins in random sizes and sprinkled across the dress with no discernible pattern.

"I love how there are more sequins around the waist that look like a belt and how they gather all around the hem of the dress too," I said.

"There're such pretty colors, too," Khloe said. "White, black, gray."

"I'm so, so happy we found it. Add it to the cart before it disappears!" Khloe selected my size and put the dress in our cart. We found shoes and clutches to match our dresses before placing the order with my emergency credit card. I'd already asked Mom and Dad if I could use it for my party outfit and Khloe's, and they'd agreed. Khloe, though, had insisted on paying me back.

I let out a giant sigh, happy that my dress was ordered. Khloe sent the e-mail with dress links to Lex, Clare, and, Jill.

"Now we get to pick out masks," I said.

Khloe wiggled her eyebrows. "I think we should do them on our own computers and not show them to each other until we get dressed on party night."

"I love that idea! The party *is* supposed to have mystery, after all."

6

BIRTHDAY GENIE

KHLOE PLUGGED IN HER IPAD TO CHARGE and grabbed her party planning notebook. "Before I look for my mask," she said, "mind if we talk details?"

"Of course!"

"For space, I'm going to ask someone in administration whom I need to speak with about booking the ballroom for that night."

"The *ballroom*? Whoa." I tried to imagine Canterwood's stunning ballroom decorated just for me.

"Where else, silly?" Khloe asked, giggling. She kept writing. "We'll need the space. I'll talk to Zack about one of his friends DJing. We'll have room for food and drink tables, dancing, and presents in the ballroom."

"Speaking of presents, I've been thinking about that already."

"Your present wish list is my command," Khloe said. "Tell me."

"Can I?" I asked, motioning to Khloe's iPad. She handed it to me.

I opened a new tab on the Internet and typed in a Web address. I handed the iPad back to Khloe.

She stared at the screen, silent. "Um." Khloe shifted, scratching her forehead. "Laur, I know I promised you a *perfect* party, but I don't think I can make this happen. Even if all the guests and I pooled every bit of allowance we had, we can't afford a racehorse."

I burst into laughter. I laughed so hard my shoulders shook, and tears ran down my cheeks. Khloe looked at me like she was a step away from calling Christina for a straitjacket for her roomie.

"Khlo," I said, "I don't want you guys to buy me a *racehorse*! Omigosh, I'd be the biggest, most selfish brat if I asked my friends to get me a racehorse for my birthday."

Khloe shook her head. "I'm so confused."

"Did you scroll down?" I asked. "Look."

I leaned over the iPad, looking over her shoulder at

it with her. I pointed to the "Donate to Our Charity" heading.

"OH!" Khloe slapped a hand over her forehead. Now it was her turn to laugh. "You had me totally freaked! First, I thought 'Omigod, I can't get LT what she wants!' then I thought 'LT's replacing Whisper?!'"

"If I did that, it would make me the biggest snob in our grade. Probably in the whole school."

"Or all time," Khloe added, grinning.

"This is what I want more than anything, though," I said. "I have everything I need. I really do. I want to help horses who are coming off the track from injuries or age and are being retrained to be pleasure horses, companions—whatever."

"This is such a great idea. I'm not just donating on your birthday. Next time I really think I 'need' that dress from Express, I'm giving money to this charity."

"We just know how much it costs to take care of one horse. And we don't even have to worry about electricity bills, water costs, stable repairs—all of that. I can't imagine the cost of keeping a dozen or more horses and not taking a penny for them. They're all up for adoption here. It's up to the adopter how much, if anything, they donate."

Khloe wrote *Donate to horse charity* under *Presents*. "I'll make sure everyone who comes knows that this is what you want."

"Ooh, so guest list!" I said.

"I've got a special notebook for that." Khloe looked through a stack of notebooks and pulled out a pink one with glitter purple polka dots.

"Do you want an inclusive invite-only party? Or do you want to invite everyone in the seventh grade?"

"Everyone. Don't you think? It seems kind of fifth grade to not invite people, and the more people who come, the more money I'll get for charity."

Khloe made a notation. "Def agree. Plus, you pretty much know everyone in our grade, anyway!"

I got up and walked to our mini-fridge. "Soda?" I asked Khloe.

She rolled her brown eyes to the ceiling. "Umm . . . Orange Crush, please."

I grabbed a Sierra Mist and handed Khloe her soda. We popped the tops and I held up my can, motioning for Khloe to raise hers.

"To my BFFL, Khloe Kinsella. Not only the best roommate, greatest friend, and most fun person I've ever met, but a superstar party planner."

"Aww. Geeze, LT. That was so nice." We clinked our cans together. I truly couldn't have gotten a better roommate. Plus, Khloe knew how to make a party Canterwood worthy—something I didn't feel confident I could do on my own yet. The last thing I wanted was a birthday celebration faux pas.

"Since we know we're going to invite everyone and we just talked about guests, want to work on the invitation?" Khloe asked.

"Love to."

"I don't want to wait too long, because I have to order the invitations from Print Factory and I want to make sure the paper quality is perfect, the font is what we want, and that the colors aren't off."

I touched Khloe's arm. "Hey, I don't want you spending money on this. I figured we'd do e-vites and my parents would cover decorations and anything I wanted. You shouldn't spend *your* money, Khlo. You're doing more than enough by organizing the party."

Khloe held up a hand. She pointed to it. "Talk to this. Take a deep breath and repeat after me, 'I, Lauren Towers, am relinquishing all control of my party to the very capable blonde with ultraglossy hair. I am only allowed to help when asked by aforementioned shiny-haired girl.'"

I was laughing before Khloe even finished.

"I—" I couldn't get the words out; I was laughing too hard.

She stared at me, raising an eyebrow. "What is *so* funny, missy? The part that I'm very capable? Or . . ." Khloe mock-gasped and covered her mouth. She widened her eyes, looking horrified. "That I don't have gleaming hair?"

I giggled harder, and Khloe grinned. Bowing my head, I held up both hands, palms facing Khloe. "I turn over all party planning aspects to my beyond-competent roommate, who has blindingly shiny hair. So much so that it rivals the sun!" I looked around the room. "Have you seen my sunglasses?"

Khloe laughed. She leaned over so she could see herself in the full-length mirror. "I do need to get a gloss treatment done. BUT, that's not the point. Let's start on the invite."

Khloe got up and grabbed her laptop. She opened the royal purple computer, and a photo of Ever made up the wallpaper. The bay mare wore a bright yellow halter that made her black points look even darker. Her ears pointed forward, and she looked happy.

"I love that picture," I said. "Where'd you take it?"

"Last year when I took Ever home for the summer. The arena behind us is the place we worked out in Boston."

"When we're not party planning, I want to hear more about your stable there. I don't know much about it."

"I'd love to tell you," Khloe said, but I could tell from her tone that she was only half paying attention to me. She opened Word, started a new document, and opened the pull-down menu for fonts. "I think something elegant. Agree?"

"Definitely. Let's look."

We huddled over her computer, scrolling through fonts.

"Nope," Khloe said.

"No." I shook my head.

"Too bold," Khloe said with wide eyes.

"Too bubblegum-y."

"Hmmm," Khloe said. "Maybe this one." She wrote the name in her notebook. "Want to pick a few and choose from those? Or even do a mock-up and change it to each font we want to try?"

"Great idea. Let's do that."

We kept looking and—

"That's it!" we shouted simultaneously.

We grinned at each other and selected the font. Together, we drafted and redrafted the invitation until it was *très parfait*.

★★ You are cordially invited ★★

To Lauren Towers's thirteenth birthday party! It's a masquerade party, so don't wear anything less than your absolute best. Saturday, October 31, at 7 p.m. will be a night of mystery, music, and more. The party will begin in the ballroom, and a few outdoor activities will be optional . . . unless you're too scared.

As a special note, if you are intending on gifting the birthday girl, she has a request: Please make a donation to Safe Haven for Thoroughbreds. No amount is too small, and all proceeds go toward caring for retired racehorses in rehabilitation.

Hope to see you on Halloween night to celebrate Lauren's turning 1-3!

RSVP to Khloe Kinsella, party planner to the stars, at khloekinsella@canterwoodcrest.com. All of those who are attending will need to e-mail with a "yes" by October 25.

We stared at the invitation, then turned to each other, slapping palms. "I love it! Khlo, you did an amazing job!"

"Thanks, L. But it was a team effort." Khloe flipped to a page in her notebook with *Invitations* written on top. She checked off *Write invitation*. "Want to log on to Print Factory and choose paper and other options?"

I nodded. "This is so much fun. Maybe I want to be a party planner. Or," I laughed, "I just love planning events for myself and my friends."

"I haven't had this much fun in a long time," Khloe said. She logged on to Print Factory, and it didn't take long for us to talk through our ideas for the invites and have a mock-up ready to send for printing.

We'd chosen black rice paper with silver text. It looked like Halloween—haunting and beautiful. I'd never seen a cooler invitation.

"I think it's good to go," I said. "Looks like it'll take a day to process, and since we're ordering so many, it'll ship in two days."

"Perf," Khloe said. "Enough time to make sure the invites are what we want and for Lex and Jill to pass them out. They volunteered to be on handout duty."

Better friends didn't exist.

"Do you want to take a break?" I asked. "Or keep

going?" I didn't want Khloe to feel like she had to work on this project forever.

"I'm *so* into this, if you are." Khloe picked up a stack of magazines and set them in front of us. "Want to decide on decorations and color scheme?"

"Hmmm . . ." I pretended to think. "Yes! I've got ideas, but nothing concrete."

Khloe got up and opened our pantry door. "Looking for candy," she explained. "I'm kind of glad, actually, that you don't have anything superspecific in mind. I'd like it to be a little bit of a surprise for you. But all while keeping the look and colors you want."

Khloe emitted a satisfied noise and pulled out bite-size Three Musketeers, mini peppermint patties, Tropical Skittles, and a king-size package of strawberry Twizzlers. She put the candy in a plastic lime-green bowl we'd found online at Target and put it between us as she sat down. She opened and bit into a peppermint patty as I opened the Tropical Skittles and put a few in my mouth.

Khloe picked up a different notebook—this one silver with hearts—and wrote *Decorations* across the top of the first page.

"Tell me everything that comes to mind—colors, furniture, even food, I guess—and it'll give me an idea of what you want. Or if you've seen a party that you loved in a movie or read about it in a book, tell me and I'll rent the movie or read the book."

I tilted my head to smile at her. "You do realize you're the best roommate at Canterwood, right? I can't even begin to *try* to tell you what this means to me."

"Oh, don't try," Khloe said. "Save it for later when I need favors." She winked. "Okay, go."

I took a breath. "I'm thinking about the color scheme being deep purple, black, silver, and a touch of orange. The orange wouldn't have to be anything more than a few pumpkins in the room, but I think it'll add that Halloween ambience we want."

Nodding, Khloe kept writing.

"Nothing like streamers or 'Happy Birthday' banners. I want the feel to be incredibly glam. Everyone will be dressed up, and I think the ballroom should reflect the clothes. It should feel so luxurious."

"You mentioned pumpkins," Khloe said. "Maybe we don't carve them, but instead leave some orange, and get some spray paint. We could paint some silver and purple, and a few could be orange with a clear glittery glaze."

"That's a great idea!"

Khloe and I talked through the rest of the decorations,

and I left most of the final decisions up to her. That made Khlo happy, because she was set on having as much as possible of the party a surprise.

"Last detail for now," Khloe said. "Cake."

"What do you think about cupcakes?" I asked, uncrossing my legs and stretching. "More specifically, strawberry cupcakes with vanilla icing."

"A girl who knows what she wants. Love it," Khloe said. She finishing writing and closed her notebook, and we smiled at each other.

"I can't thank you enough," I said. "You're going to do a crazy-awesome job. Can it be Halloween already?"

"Um, no. I need a least a *few* days to get this put together, thank you." Khloe stood, reaching out to pull me up with her. "Now you have to wait and I get to plan!"

I hadn't been this excited about my birthday in a long time. I felt like a little kid waiting for Christmas. It wasn't going to be easy not to peek at what Khloe was doing. But I had to be a good roommate and respect her privacy. Unless a notebook, somehow, *fell* open in front of me, I was going to have to wait three long weeks.

7

ALWAYS FORGET
YOUR UMBRELLA

RAIN PELTED THE ENGLISH BUILDING, causing tiny streams to run down the sidewalks. Of course it would pour like this on a Monday. I stood inside with Clare, students passing us and opening umbrellas when they stepped outside. A mini umbrella peeked out of Clare's purple-and-white-striped messenger bag.

"This is what Khloe and I get for *not* checking the weather this morning," I said.

Clare made a face. "No umbrella?"

"Nope. Neither of us brought one."

"Give me your phone," Clare said, holding out her hand. "I'm downloading an app for you."

I fished my BlackBerry out of my bag and handed it to

her. "Ooh, do you know about one that'll turn my phone into a raincoat?"

Clare smiled, clicking a few buttons, then handed me the phone. "Unfortunately, it won't help you this time. But it *will* chime with a heads-up the next time it's about to rain."

"Thanks! That's so cool."

Clare and I smiled at each other. Things had been so different between us—among all of us—since Riley's sudden departure last week. Clare and I hadn't had much time to hang out one on one. In the time we had spent together, Clare had been a different girl. Like now—she was funny, smart, superfriendly, and not waiting for Riley to come along and tell her what to do or make her feel bad for talking to Khloe or me.

"Maybe you, Khloe, and I can all fit under my umbrella," Clare said, taking it out. I looked at the sky-blue umbrella dotted with tiny colorful somethings.

"What are those?" I peered closer.

"Oh, check it." Clare undid the snap and shook out the umbrella. It was covered in My Little Ponies.

"Aw! It's so you!" I said. It reminded me off the stuffed ponies and other animals on Clare's bed.

"I was so excited when I found it at Target," Clare said.

She blushed, shaking her head. "I actually bought two—the other's at home—in case this one gets blown out."

We both giggled. "I would do the same if I found something that cool."

Clare put down her stuff, freeing her hands. She twisted her long red waves into a messy bun.

"My hair's going to be three times this size when I go outside," she said. "Humidity. Awesome."

I groaned. "Tell me about it. Oh! I've got this EBT—essential beauty trick—that helps. I'll BBM it to you after class."

"Major hearts!"

The hallway was almost empty now. I realized Clare and I had been talking nonstop since we'd left English. With Riley out of the equation, Clare and I suddenly seemed to have more to talk about.

So . . . ," I started, then stopped. "I don't want to pry or anything, but how are you?"

Clare leaned on her shoulder against the wall. She took a breath, and I knew that she understood *exactly* what I was asking. "You're not prying. We're becoming better friends, and friends talk about this stuff." Clare rubbed her forehead. "It's been tough. Confusing. Not anything that I expected, so I guess that's what's making it so complicated. Riley was my best friend. I can't remember a time when we weren't doing everything together at Canterwood."

I nodded, my heart panging with sympathy for Clare.

"I think . . ." Clare paused. Her blue eyes got a far-away look in them for a moment before she focused on me again. "I think that all of our time together was part of the problem. It blinded me, sort of, to the bad side of Riley. And the bad side was *really* bad. She hurt a lot of people—you, Khloe—I'm having a hard time letting that go."

"I hope you're not blaming yourself," I said. "It's easy to get so wrapped up in someone that you don't see what's really going on."

Clare gave me a tiny smile. "Thanks. I know I didn't do those things, but I was a bystander for a lot of them. It makes me guilty too. I have to accept some blame for that."

I nodded. "Only if you let go of it at some point. Have you talked to Riley?"

Clare shifted, pressing her lips together. "No. It's so crazy—I just talked to you about how many awful things Riley did, but this other part of me wants to hear from her. She hasn't even *tried* to call, or text, or e-mail—nothing."

"No matter what, she was still your best friend," I said. "You wouldn't be human if you didn't miss her. Riley wasn't all bad, and most of the time you two spent together, I'm betting, was good. Otherwise, you wouldn't have been her friend."

Clare was quiet. For a long time. I waited, not pushing her to talk. Clare's bottom lip wobbled, and she looked like she was fighting back tears. She kept her gaze on the marble floor.

I reached out, putting a hand on her forearm.

Seconds ticked by before Clare let out a big breath and met my eyes. "Thank you."

"Anytime," I said. "I hope we get to be better friends."

A real smile came over Clare's face. "Me too." The smile turned into a teasing grin. "Now I'm even more excited that Khloe recruited me for the 'LT B-day Team.'"

"The *what*?"

"Oh, nothing. Just Lexa, Jill, me, you know, *people*, who are helping Khloe plan your birthday party. But I can't say anything else."

"You're *so* mean!" I rolled my eyes, pretending to be serious. "If you want to become friends faster . . . you could tell me everything. It would be our secret." I gave Clare my sweetest smile.

"Aw, Lauren Towers." Clare shook her head. "I didn't think you'd stoop so low."

We both cracked up, turning as sneakers squeaked down the hallway.

"Omigod!" Khloe hurried up to us, papers almost trailing out of her bag and books stuffed with notes in her arms. "Mr. Davidson acted like I personally insulted him! Plus, he talked so long, he almost made us miss lunch. You guys were so sweet to wait for me."

"Why was he upset?" Clare asked.

"We were *both* in class with you," I said. "You didn't do anything."

Khloe frowned. "I turned in the homework, and I didn't do any of the extra-credit work. Hello, it's *optional*, and I didn't have time. Mr. D was all, 'You had the ability to answer these questions, Khloe. You have more potential than you're utilizing.'"

Clare scrunched her lightly freckled nose. "Mr. D's usually so chill. Sorry he freaked on you."

I nodded. "He should have made those questions a requirement if he wanted them answered, then. Not an option."

Khloe rolled her eyes and looked outside. "Geeze. Good-bye pretty blowout."

"Clare has an umbrella, and she offered to share," I said. "You guys stay dry under the My Little Ponies and I'll make a run for it."

"No way," Khloe said. "I'm not letting you get soaked alone. We'll both go together, and it'll give me an excuse to try a couple of updos and braids for wet hair."

"And it's not like we're witches and we'll melt," I said, giggling. "Let's do it."

Khloe smiled, linking her arm through mine.

"You guys have some invisible rain shield that I can't see?"

I turned, pulling Khloe with me, and saw Drew.

"Obviously, linking arms gives us superpowers," I said.

Drew had an amused smile on his face as he stopped in front of us. He looked supercute in a white T-shirt, dark wash jeans, and Chucks. A black messenger bag was slung across his chest.

"Well." Drew leaned closer to us, whispering. "I wouldn't want anyone to find out about your powers and expose you two. Laur, what if you come under my umbrella with me?" He produced a black one from his bag. "And we'll all go to the caf together?"

"I think we shouldn't risk revealing our powers," Khloe said, mock seriously. She unlinked her arm from mine and stepped next to Clare. "Let's go!"

We stepped outside. and Drew popped open his umbrella. We looked at each other, then, laughing, we dashed through the rain. My shoulder bumped against Drew's as we dodged puddles. I wished the cafeteria was farther away. I didn't care about my hair, or clothes, or how I looked from the rain. I got to be with Drew.

"I'm *not* sorry you forgot your umbrella," Drew said, slowing as we approached the caf stairs. His bluer than blue eyes looked at me. I hated him—just a little!—for making me a tongue-tied, flustered mess.

I smiled—the words coming easily. "Me either."

8

WHISPER'S NEW NAME: TROUBLEMAKER

"WISP!" I PUT WHISPER'S TACK DOWN ON her glossy wooden trunk outside of her stall. Whisper, my *très belle* gray mare, had her head hanging over the stall door. She reached her black muzzle with a pink-and-white snip toward me.

"Hi," I said, kissing her satiny muzzle and rubbing her cheek. "I don't know about your day, but mine was *super*long. At least I'm here now, and I'm so excited for our lesson."

Yesterday Mr. Conner had us practice dressage in the outdoor arena. Today, for Tuesday's session, he'd sent an e-mail notifying us that the lesson would be indoors.

I picked up Whisper's grooming kit and unlatched her stall door. She stepped forward, starting out of the stall.

"Hey, whoa!" I said, grabbing her halter. I tugged on it, putting pressure on her nose and halting her. "You're not allowed to leave the stall without me. You know better." My firm tone made Whisper lower her head.

I backed her up into her stall and shut the door behind us. "We're staying inside now." I balanced the tack box on the stall door and plucked one of Whisper's cotton lead lines off the hook near her stall door.

I clipped the pink lead to her halter ring, tying her to an iron bar on the front of her stall. "You tried to make a break for it yesterday, too. Are you that eager to go work out?" I shook my head. I'd have to talk to Mike and Doug about Whisper's new trick. I wanted to be sure the grooms who cared for her knew what she'd been trying. They'd be able to help me break Whisper of the bad habit or report back if she didn't try it with them.

I loved grooming almost as much as I did riding. Grooming always felt intimate to me—like it connected me more with my horse. It was one-on-one time where I could talk to Whisper and have body contact with brushes and massages, and where neither of us had to be focused on a lesson or movement.

I rummaged through Whisper's tack box—blue plastic with glitter—and found a rubber currycomb. I slid the purple oval-shaped brush onto my hand and stepped up to Whisper's shoulder. It had been a few days since I'd curried her—she didn't need it every day, since she was groomed daily. Starting at her poll, I moved the currycomb in small circles with light pressure. I went over her neck, shoulder, back, barrel, and rump, then switched sides.

"You'd think I never brushed you," I told Whisper. Little clumps of gray hair filled the comb's teeth and fell to the sawdust below my feet.

After I'd curried both sides, I switched to a dandy brush. I flicked the stiff-bristled brush over the same spots I'd curried. Neither the currycomb nor the dandy brush were meant for sensitive areas of a horse such as the face or legs.

I still remembered learning that information before my first riding lesson. When the groom—I couldn't think of her name—had told me I could hurt a horse by currying the face, I'd been terrified at the thought of hurting my horse. I'd barely touched the currycomb to the little bay I'd been assigned and only curried the barrel so I wouldn't get anywhere near any sensitive spots. The groom, a college-aged girl, took about three or four sessions with me before she was able to convince me to curry more of the horse. I shook my head at the memory.

Whisper sighed, relaxed. She cocked her left back hoof, resting. "I'm glad you calmed down a little, missy," I said. "I was starting to think someone had fed you sugar cubes while I'd been at class."

I tossed the dandy brush into the tack box and grabbed the body brush. "This is your favorite one," I said to my sleepy mare. "You better start waking up, 'cause I'm almost done. You can sleep after our lesson and your cooldown. Lucky!" I patted her. "I've got to go back to my room and do homework."

Soon Whisper was groomed and tacked up. I led her out of the stall—she stayed behind me like she was supposed to and stopped while I put on my helmet. We walked down the aisle and stopped inside the entrance of the indoor arena.

I'd taken longer than usual to groom Whisper, and everyone was already warming up in the arena.

"Everyone" now meant Cole, Clare, Lexa, and Drew. No Riley. It had been strange not to have her at yesterday's lesson. I wasn't going to lie and say I missed her. The lesson had been *different*. Much less stressful.

I gathered the reins in my left hand, stuck my toe in the stirrup iron, and bounced lightly on my right foot. I lowered myself into the saddle and started to adjust my right stirrup. Whisper, without any signal from me, took off at a fast walk toward the other horses.

"Whoa." I used the same low, firm tone as I had when she'd tried to leave her stall without me. I tugged once, sharply, on the reins. Whisper stopped, tossing her head and raising her muzzle into the air, trying to avoid the bit. I kept pressure on her mouth and sat deep in the saddle. We weren't going anywhere until *I* told Whisper to move.

Everyone else kept their horses at the other end of the arena, seeing that I was working with Whisper.

I made her stand, watching the other horses move while I adjusted my stirrup. Then I pretended I needed to fix my other one. Whisper's muscles rippled and she shifted her weight, ears pointed toward the other horses. Drew and Clare had their horses trotting in circles. Lexa had halted Honor and was stretching in the saddle. Cole and Valentino walked along the arena's edge.

Now you can join your friends, I wanted to say to Whisper. A lot of my friends talked to their horses during lessons, but I didn't. Not unless it was praise or a reprimand like I'd given Whisper earlier.

Instead of allowing Whisper to walk directly toward the other horses, I eased up on the reins and tightened my legs ever so slightly against her sides. I pulled the left rein, guiding Whisper into a turn *away* from the horses. I could *feel* her indecision beneath me about whether to fight me or go along with what I asked.

Whisper turned in the direction I asked, both of her ears tilted back at me, but she faced the other end of the arena and walked toward the rain. We weren't joining the rest of the team until she changed her attitude. Hello, angry ears!

We stayed at the opposite end of the giant arena and started our warm-up. I guided Whisper through walking, trotting, circles, and finally, she had no resistance in her body. An ear flicked back to me, signaling that she was paying attention. The other ear pointed forward—happy.

I stroked her shoulder. "Good girl," I said, wanting her to know she deserved praise. Instead of turning her away from the group as I had been when we reached a certain point, I let her continue to walk toward the other horses. Her walk got a notch faster, but Wisp stayed on her best behavior. She seemed to know that we'd end up at the other side of the arena, alone, if she acted up.

I guided her beside Drew and Polo. Drew seemed finished with his warm-up and was walking his gelding.

"Are you being a troublemaker?" Drew asked Whisper.

"She definitely was," I said. "I think she's on her best behavior now, though. Or at least, I hope she is."

Drew smiled. He'd paired a navy T-shirt with black breeches and paddock boots. Dark blue was one of my favorite colors on him—it made his pale skin stand out.

"You did good work with her," Drew said. "I wouldn't have thought to keep Polo at the opposite end of the arena if he'd acted like that."

His words made my heart beat a little faster. "Thanks. If I hadn't, Whisper would have gotten her way. She was a bit of a handful before our lesson, so I had to be sure she got it that I'm in charge."

"What happened before?" Drew asked.

We kept the horses walking at an easy pace around the perimeter of the arena. I told him about earlier, and Drew gave me some tips. I lost myself in conversation with him. I didn't even know that I'd gone on rider autopilot, or that other people and horses were in the arena.

"Please bring your horses to the center!" Mr. Conner's voice made me jump.

Drew had been telling me about a bad habit Polo had picked up last summer and how he'd broken it. I glanced at him to see if he'd noticed my reaction. If he had, he was being cool about it and not busting me.

"Talk more later?" I asked.

"Most definitely," Drew said.

That made cliché butterflies flitter in my stomach. I walked Whisper to the center of the arena, smiling at Cole, Lex, and Clare. They did the same back, but I recognized a *look* on their faces. It was a *you were totally absorbed in talking to Drew* look.

We lined up in front of Mr. Conner and halted our horses. The butterflies over Drew flew away. All of my attention was on Whisper.

Mr. Conner was here now, and I didn't want her moving one hoof wrong in front of him. I never wanted Mr. Conner to think Whisper and I weren't ready to be on his intermediate team. The six-foot-something instructor with inky black cropped hair was tough on riders during lessons, but always had our best interest in mind. He'd been compassionate and understanding toward me when Whisper and I had started at Canterwood last month. It made me never want to disappoint him.

"Good afternoon, class," Mr. Conner said. He had his usual clipboard and pen in hand. "I want to speak with you about something before we begin."

I forced myself to keep my eyes on Mr. Conner and not look at Drew, on my left, or Clare to my right.

"Prior to yesterday's class," Mr. Conner began, "I spoke briefly about the departure of one of our teammates, Riley Edwards. I'm sure you, as well as I, are wishing Riley well at her new venture."

I bit my tongue so I wouldn't roll my eyes.

"Riley's sudden departure from Canterwood has left us with the opportunity for a new rider to join the team," Mr. Conner said, moving his dark-brown eyes from student to student. "At this time, I've decided to leave the seventh-grade intermediate team with five members."

Yes! I glanced over at Drew, who met my eyes and smiled. I loved our new team.

"If I decide to consider an additional student, you will be informed," Mr. Conner said. "For now, keeping you as a group of five has many advantages—one of which being that I will have more time for each individual. I look forward to working more closely with you and your horses."

"Thank you, Mr. Conner," Lexa said.

"Yes, thanks," Cole said. The rest of us chimed in with our thanks.

Mr. Conner laughed. "Oh, I don't know if I'd thank me just yet. You may very well wish there was another student back on the team after a few weeks of more individualized attention."

Clare, Lexa, Drew, Cole, and I laughed too.

"All right, let's begin," Mr. Conner said. "This is going to be the first of a new type of lesson. Four of you will be working in pairs, and one of you will be training with me for the session. With an odd number of riders, I will work with a different student one-on-one whenever we have a lesson that requires pairing."

Ooh! So exciting and nerve-racking at the same time. Training with Mr. Conner—and *only* Mr. Conner—was huge. It was like a private lesson. It also made me a little nervous, because whenever it was my turn, all of his attention would be on Whisper and me. I definitely didn't want to mess up even the tiniest bit.

"For the pairs, I'd like Clare and Lauren and Drew and Cole," Mr. Conner said. "Lexa, you'll be working with me."

Clare and I smiled at each other. We'd never been partners.

"One of you will dismount, go grab a lunge line and lunge halter, and give your horse to Mike or Doug," Mr. Conner explained. "They're waiting for your horses and will be walking them along the side aisles until they are needed."

"The person on the ground will instruct the rider through lunge exercises that I'll call out," Mr. Conner continued. "After one person has completed the set of exercises, you'll switch roles. Though I'll be working with Lexa, I'll still be watching each pair."

I sneaked a glance down at Lex. She saw me and gave me a *yikes!* face with wide eyes.

"Partner up and get one of your horses hooked up to a lunge line," Mr. Conner instructed. "Then we'll begin."

"You can ride first if you want," I said, twisting in the saddle to face Clare.

She nodded. "Sounds good. I'm glad we're partners. It's going to be fun."

"Me too. And I'll reserve comment on the 'fun' part until I hear what Mr. Conner's going to make us do," I said, lowering my voice so he couldn't hear me.

Clare laughed. "Point."

"Be right back!"

I dismounted and led Whisper out of the arena, with Cole and Valentino just behind us. I stopped outside the arena, waiting for him.

"Do you hate me for getting Drew?" Cole asked. He peeked at me from behind Valentino's neck.

I smiled. "Nah. I'd be too distracted if we were partners. Plus, Clare and I are becoming better friends. I'm glad we're working together."

"That's really great," Cole said. His words radiated with sincerity. "Riley's leaving is going to make things so much better for you and your friends—especially Khloe and Clare's friendship."

"I can't see how it won't be good for everyone. Riley hasn't even been gone a week and I've talked to Clare more since Friday than I ever have."

Cole and I walked the horses forward, spotting Mike and Doug scrubbing saddles in the aisle. Thanking the grooms, we handed them our horses' reins and hurried to the tack room. Mr. Conner was probably counting the seconds we were gone.

9

CLARE MINUS RILEY = AWESOME

CLARE AND FUEGO TROTTED AROUND ME IN A circle, Clare's arms out by her sides. It hadn't taken long to put the lunge halter on Fuego. I'd fed out enough line so the chestnut could move in a medium-size circle. Mr. Conner had made sure we all knew how to lunge horses, then had given Cole and me instructions to tell our riders.

"Sitting trot," I called to Clare. "Keep your arms out to the sides and leave your reins down." Clare nodded and posted for another beat before sitting. This was the first time I'd really had to put all of my attention on Clare's riding. She was *good*. Really good. Her chemistry with Fuego was undeniable—he was fiery, but listened to Clare. She balanced him out by being calm and unflappable.

"Can you deepen your seat?" I said. "It looks like you're bouncing just a little."

At first I'd been so hesitant about giving Clare instruction. But she'd responded positively to all of my constructive criticism, and it felt like when her turn was over, Clare wouldn't be mad at me because she'd felt picked on by me. It was scary, too, to tell a fellow teammate what to do. I didn't have Mr. Conner's background and knowledge. What if I told Clare to fix something that wasn't wrong?

Trust yourself, I thought. *At least a little. You're not telling Clare to change everything about the way she rides. You've got to trust your gut.*

Within a couple of strides, Clare's seat was tighter. That made me feel more confident about the validity of my suggestion.

I moved with Fuego, turning slowly in a circle as he moved. "That looks *perfect*, Clare! You're going with Fuego now."

Clare smiled. "Pick up your reins and bring Fuego to a walk, then halt," I said. "We'll change direction."

Clare picked up her knotted reins and slowed Fuego. I gathered the lunge line in my hand as I walked toward them—making sure not to wrap it around my hand. Mr. Conner had warned all of us never to do that in case the horse we were working with spooked and we could be pulled to the ground or dragged.

I stepped up to Fuego, patting his shoulder. Clare smiled down at me. "That was fun *and* hard," she said. "You're a good instructor, Lauren."

"Whew," I said. "I'm so glad you said that! I was worried you might be annoyed or mad from any critiquing that I gave you."

Clare waved a hand at me. "Omigosh, no way. Everything you said was right, and it's not like you were screaming, 'Clare! You totally suck and give up now!' while I rode."

We giggled.

"It *did* cross my mind . . . ," I teased, grinning.

Clare rolled her big blue eyes, pretending to be horrified. "Seriously, I want you to feel free to say whatever you're thinking. This is practice, and we're here to learn from each other. Plus, if you're mean to me . . ." Now she grinned. "I'm lunging *you* next."

"And with that, let's go the other way," I said. We smiled at each other and got Fuego started at a walk in the opposite direction.

I put Clare and Fuego through a variety of moves that Mr. Conner had suggested. Watching them made me proud to have them as teammates.

Cole, spaced away from us and Lexa and Mr. Conner, had Drew trotting with no stirrups. Lexa was halted, and Mr. Conner was speaking to her.

Mr. Conner walked over to me, not saying anything as I continued to coach Clare.

"Bring Fuego to a walk, cross your stirrups over your saddle, and drop the reins," I said. "Then walk for a half circle before trotting."

"I've been watching you and Clare," Mr. Conner said.

I grasped the lunge line tighter. *Please say we're doing a good job!* I thought.

"How does it feel to be instructing?" Mr. Conner asked. "Is Clare responding to your feedback, and do you feel free to speak up if you notice any areas for improvements?"

"I love instructing," I said, keeping my gaze on Clare as I spoke. "It was harder than I thought at the beginning. I was nervous about saying anything to her about places for her to improve. She made every change that I suggested, though." I took a breath, hoping I was telling Mr. Conner the right things. "I talked to Clare about my earlier fear when we changed directions, and she was amazing—she wants my feedback."

Mr. Conner nodded. I kept the lunge line taut and kept moving in a slow circle, Mr. Conner moving with me.

"Why were you anxious about giving Clare feedback?" Mr. Conner asked.

I took a long pause before answering. "Walk," I called to Clare, then I glanced at Mr. Conner. "I'm on the same team as Clare. I'm not a trained instructor like you. What if I *thought* something that needed improvement was wrong?"

"What else?" Mr. Conner asked. "It feels like there's more."

His tone was low, so only I could hear him. He spoke gently, too. It made me feel more comfortable talking to him.

"I was scared, too, that Clare would take my comments as attacks and be mad," I said. "But it's not that way at all. Mainly, I was-slash-am concerned that I'll give Clare the wrong instructions."

"Lauren," Mr. Conner said, causing me to look at him for a second. His usually stern face looked softened. "You have every right to be worried that Clare, one of your peers, might take your instruction poorly. As you've commented and as Clare's demonstrated, however, that's not the case. I'm proud that you spoke to her about your fear regarding that matter."

"Thank you," I said. I kept Clare at a walk while Mr. Conner spoke to me.

"It's also normal that you felt your input about Clare's skills could be detrimental to her riding," Mr. Conner continued. "Keep in mind that I asked all of you to do this exercise for a reason. *I* trust each of my intermediate team riders to coach the others. I want you to believe in your own skills enough to have the trust in yourself that I do."

The last sentence made me look up at him. "You really trust *me* like that?"

Mr. Conner smiled. "You haven't given me a reason not to. Lauren, as a rider on this team, I hope to build up your self-confidence. If we combine a healthy level of confidence with your talents as a rider, you will be well on your way to accomplishing great things."

I wished Khloe, Lexa, or *anyone* had been around to hear what Mr. Conner had just said. I half believed I'd heard him wrong.

"Thank you," I managed to get out. "I'll work on that."

Mr. Conner smiled, patting my shoulder. "That's what I hoped you'd say. Keep up the good work." He looked at Clare. "Nice job, Clare. You're executing strong, beautiful movements."

Clare beamed. "Thanks, Mr. Conner!"

"I'll be watching to see how you handle lunging."

Mr. Conner gave both of us a quick nod and headed at a brisk walk over to Drew and Cole.

Both grinning, Clare and I gave each other a thumbs-up. Mr. Conner's words stayed with me as I put Clare and Fuego through more exercises. *He trusts you,* I thought, watching Clare's two-point position. *You've got to start trusting yourself.*

"Please switch roles, everyone!" Mr. Conner called.

Clare eased Fuego to a walk from the working trot they'd been doing, and I gathered the lunge line in my hands.

I looked behind me at Lexa. She noticed me looking and, checking to be sure Mr. Conner wasn't looking, stuck out her tongue and mouthed, *Tired.*

I stuck out my bottom lip. *Sorry,* I mouthed back.

Lexa smiled. *Sweet Shoppe,* she mouthed. It took me a couple of seconds to realize what she meant before I nodded, smiling back.

Clare halted Fuego in front of me and dismounted. Her freckled cheeks were pink, and a few tendrils of curly red hair had escaped from her ponytail.

"Thank you, Instructor Lauren," Clare said, her tone playful. "You gave us quite a workout." She patted her horse's shoulder. "I mean it, though, thank you for being so thoughtful with your comments. You pointed out a few things that I've been struggling with, and I need to devote more time to them. I hope I can give you the level of critique you gave me."

"Clare, geeze," I said. "Wow. Thank you for saying that. It means more to me than you know. I had fun playing Mr. Conner, and I'm sure you will too. And *please*. You're going to give me amazing feedback—I want to know everything that needs work. Honest."

"Okay," Clare said. "Like you, I was feeling nervous about critiquing you. I don't want to hurt your feelings or anything."

"Remember what you told me?" I asked. "Just don't say 'Lauren! You totally suck and give up now!' and we'll be fine."

We laughed, and Clare nodded. She took the lunge halter off Fuego as Mike magically appeared with Whisper in tow. I thanked him as he handed her reins to me, then took Fuego from Clare.

Clare motioned for me to look in the other direction. Redheaded Doug was swapping Valentino for Polo. "Do Mike and Doug have secret cell phones or *something* so they're always ready to help when we need them?"

"I've wondered about that too," I said. "Maybe they

have ESP and sense it when Mr. Conner needs them."

I slipped off Whisper's bridle, put on the lunge halter, and then put her bridle back on. Clare clipped the lunge line to a ring on the bridle as I mounted.

"Ready?" Clare asked.

"Ready."

10

MY TURN

CLARE FED OUT LINE AS I MOVED WHISPER
away from her. Whisper moved smoothly beneath me at a
walk, her strides long and rhythmic.

"Drop your reins, keep your hands off Whisper, and
trot," Clare called.

I let the leather reins rest on Wisp, held my hands just
above the saddle's pommel, and squeezed my legs against
Whisper's sides. She moved quickly from a walk to a trot.
I eased up the pressure from my legs and posted. We made
several circles around Clare. Whisper stretched her neck,
and her ears started flicking back and forth. *Uh-oh.*

Whisper realized she had more rein. Her legs moved
faster as she slowly sped up her trot. It was as if Whisper
was smart enough to realize she was doing something

wrong, so she tried to keep me from noticing the faster pace.

"Lauren, pick up your reins and get Whisper back to her original pace," Clare said. "Make her do a few circles at that speed, then drop your reins again. We'll see if Whisper takes advantage of you again or not."

I nodded, letting Clare know I'd heard her, and picked up the reins. I did a half halt and deepened my seat. Whisper quickly slowed to a smoother trot—the speed we'd started at. I kept pressure on the reins for a few circles. Whisper kept the same pace and didn't try to move faster. Instead of dropping the reins all at once, I gradually gave Whisper more and more rein, making sure she stayed at an even trot before gently resting them on her neck.

"Great idea," Clare said. "Nice trick. Let's see if Whisper notices this time."

As we circled Clare, I kept my body posture relaxed and held my hands over Whisper as if I was holding invisible reins. This time, we made it through the exercise without a problem.

"Pick up your reins, but lose the stirrups," Clare said.

I crossed the stirrups in front of me so they wouldn't bang against Whisper's sides and held the reins.

"Sitting trot for three circles," Clare instructed.

• • •

"Time's up, everyone. Please come to the center of the arena." Mr. Conner's voice startled me. I'd been fully focused on Clare and Whisper.

"Yay!" Clare said. "Great job, LT!"

I halted Whisper and dismounted, patting her neck as Clare hurried up to us.

"Thank you, Clare," I said. "You were an awesome instructor. I really appreciate everything you pointed out to me. I know we had a good workout because I'm *so* sore!"

"Sorry!" Clare said, giggling.

She unclipped the lunge line and helped me take off the halter and slip the bridle back over Whisper's head.

Together, we walked over to Mr. Conner. A *very* tired-looking Lex walked Honor over to us and stopped beside Clare. Drew and Cole fell into the lineup.

"Excellent work, class," Mr. Conner said, smiling. "If you don't have your horse, Mike or Doug are waiting outside the arena with your mounts. They'll have been cooled and are ready to be groomed."

Whisper needed a good cooldown before I groomed her. I hadn't been kidding when I'd said Clare had worked us hard.

"As a reminder, you should all be following the

reading schedule for your horse manual," Mr. Conner said. "Starting now, be prepared for a pop quiz at the beginning of any lesson. If you do not pass, you will *not* ride during that lesson. Instead you'll go back to your dorm room to read the pages again."

Major yikes! I was so lucky that Mr. Conner hadn't quizzed us today without warning. I'd been so swamped with schoolwork that I'd let the reading for lessons slide.

Drew raised his hand, and Mr. Conner nodded at him. "What happens at the next lesson?" Drew asked. "Do we get to retake the quiz?"

"Yes, after skipping one lesson, you'll take a makeup quiz with different questions covering the same material," Mr. Conner said. "If you pass, you'll be allowed to participate in the day's lesson. If not, you will skip the next two lessons before you will be given a chance to be retested."

I frowned. I understood that equine care and health was vital to being a successful rider. Plus, I wanted to know everything possible to keep Whisper healthy, happy, and in top shape. But this new skipping a lesson if we didn't pass Mr. Conner's quizzes didn't seem fair. Did he know how much schoolwork and assigned reading we had for every other class?

"If there are more questions," Mr. Conner said, "please

come see me after my next class. Or e-mail me. I will be sending an e-mail with the consequences regarding failing quizzes and other details that will hopefully answer any questions you may have." He marked off something on his clipboard and looked at us. "I'll meet you and your horses in the large outdoor arena tomorrow. Good work."

With that, he left the arena. He left five tired riders who glanced at each other, sharing the same look: *More work on top of everything else.* I think sleep was the only thing left to cut down in my schedule.

SASHA SILVER 2.0

I WOKE WITH THE SUN ON THURSDAY MORNING.
As it started to cast light over the campus, I pulled on
black yoga pants, a pale pink T-shirt, and my black Nikes
with sky-blue laces. There was just enough light peeking
through the curtains for me to leave the lights off and let
Khloe sleep. Her blond hair was spread across her zebra-
print pillow and she was on her side, hugging her unicorn
Pillow Pet.

Drew and I'd had lunch together yesterday, and we
talked about how stressed we both were. I brought up our
shared love of running, and Drew asked me to run with
him this morning before classes.

I quietly closed the bathroom door behind me and
turned on the light. Eyedrops helped take the sleepiness

out of my eyes, and I pulled my long hair into a high ponytail. A splash of cool water on my face felt refreshing.

Then it hit me.

Hard.

I was going running with *Drew Adams. Oh, mon Dieu!* What if I couldn't keep up with him? Or what if he was the slow one? *Stop, stop, stop,* I told myself. *Do you really believe* Drew *is going to be slow?* I shook my head at myself.

I squeezed a dime-size dollop of Neutrogena moisturizer with sunscreen into my hand and quickly rubbed it onto my face.

I turned off the bathroom light, grabbed my yellow-and-green rubber SLAP Watch, and tiptoed out the door. Khloe didn't move as I shut the door behind me. She'd been up later than me last night. After homework, she'd claimed to be working on lines for *Beauty and the Beast.* That would have made sense, because Khloe *was* taking over Riley's role of Belle instead of playing Mrs. Potts. But I'd caught a glimpse of a paper Khloe was writing on and saw *birthday* on it.

"I don't remember 'birthday' being in *any* of Belle's lines," I'd said to her last night.

Khloe had given me a guilty grin. "Um," she'd said,

her voice *veeery* high. "You wouldn't remember it. It's an addition to the play."

I'd stared at Khloe. And stared. And stared.

She'd burst into giggles, holding up her hands. "Okay, okay! I'm obvi not working on the play. I'm working on my roomie and BFFL's birthday plans."

"Can I see?" I'd made puppy-dog eyes. "Pleeease, KK. Just one tiny hint?"

Khloe had grasped the papers to her chest. "Nope! And don't puppy-dog-eye me, Lauren Towers. You know way too much already. Stay on your side of the room or I'll be forced to call security."

I'd snorted. "*Security*? You mean, Christina? Like, 'Christina, help! My roommate is trying to look at my secret papers. Cuff Lauren and take her to Hawthorne jail immediately!'"

Khloe had made a serious face. "Exactly. That's what I'll do."

We'd laughed and I'd let her alone, only occasionally pretending that I was going to pounce onto her bed and grab a paper.

I smiled as I walked down Hawthorne's quiet hallway. Every door was shut, and there wasn't a sound except for my footsteps on the carpet. I put on my watch, checking the time. 4:56 a.m. Perfect timing. Drew and I had agreed to meet at the fountain at five.

I opened the glass door and stepped out into the muggy air with hint of coolness. This morning, fog blanketed the campus. I couldn't see more than a few feet in front of me. Sun peeked through clouds, but it wasn't enough to burn off the fog. It was so gorgeous.

I walked toward the center of campus, taking deep breaths. My body—and mind—had missed this. Running had always been my stress reducer, but I'd had no time to run since I'd come to Canterwood. It had become apparent, though, that I would have to *make* time. Running was part of taking care of myself. I needed that to be on top of my game as a student and rider.

I sped up, squinting as I saw the courtyard come into view. I followed the sidewalk down to the center, and through the fog, someone walked toward me.

"Nice timing!" I said, smiling at Drew. We both reached the fountain at the same time.

He nodded. "No kidding."

Drew looked *très* adorable this early in the morning. His hair was a little ruffled, and he had a slight pillow-crease imprint on his left cheek. He was dressed to run in red Adidas, black pants, and a black T-shirt.

"Want to stretch here?" I asked.

"Let's do it." Drew smiled at me and put a foot on the fountain rim. He leaned forward, grabbing his ankle.

I stepped back, giving us both room. I spread my legs until I felt a slight pull from my inner thighs to my knees. Bending forward, I slowly inched my hands toward the cobblestones. My legs started to burn, so I let myself straighten, took a few seconds, and then bent forward again. This time, I was able to place my palms on the cobblestones. I repeated the stretch a couple more times.

"Do you have a set stretch routine that you always do?" Drew asked. He was stretching his hamstrings.

"Most of the time, I do the same stretches, just in a different order from the last time I ran," I said. "But if I read about a different stretch in a magazine or online, I'll try it and add it to my routine if I like it."

Drew nodded, sitting and flexing his feet. "I'm the same way. I like variety, but with stretches I know work."

I raised my right arm, bent to the left, and grabbed my left ankle. I kept my right hand pointed up and held the pose for a few seconds before switching to the other side.

"That's a cool one," Drew said.

I blushed, wiggling my toes in my shoes. I didn't know he was *watching* watching.

"It's good," I said. "You should try it sometime. I've been doing it forever."

Drew watched me do the stretch again, then mimicked me. "That feels great," he said. "Cool. I'll have to think of one to show you."

Drew and I stretched for a few more minutes before my muscles felt loose and warmed up.

"I'm set, if you are," Drew said. The pillow crease was gone from his cheek, and his eyes were wider and he looked more awake.

"I'm ready to run, Adams," I said, grinning. "You get a pass this time because you know the campus and have to show me the best running trail."

"And that's a pass *how*?" he asked as we left the courtyard.

"I have to keep pace with you and not run ahead or I'll get lost," I said. "But next time . . ." I shrugged. "I just might have to leave you behind."

"Ohhh, Lauren." Drew shook his head, his lips pressed together. "I was going to take it easy on you the first time out, but I think I have to take that back. You have to keep up with *me* or you'll get lost. I hope you brought a GPS."

We increased the speed of our walk as Drew led me toward the woods.

"Please," I said. "All I brought is this." I flashed my wrist at him. "To keep track of how long it takes you to catch me at the finish line."

Drew smiled and we both laughed.

"You're a lot of fun at five in the morning," he said. "I usually don't want to talk to anyone this early."

"I *am* a morning person. But running with a partner is going to be different. If it's anything like stretching with you, though, I think I'll like it."

We reached the edge of the woods. I recognized one of the trails I'd been on a few times with Whisper and some friends.

"Are we going on a horse trail?" I asked.

"No." Drew stopped, looking at me. "Walkers and runners are supposed to stay off the horse trails. There are usually riders on the trails either conditioning their horses, or getting a breather—something. There are too many twists and turns for people to be walking where someone could be cantering behind them."

"I'd hope I'd hear a horse coming, but . . ." My mouth formed an O. "I've usually got my iPod on."

"Exactly. That's the dangerous part. Last year one of the guys on the swim team got confused about what trail to take. He guessed and ended up on a horse trail, unknowingly. He was walking to catch his breath and he had music blasting."

"Uh-oh," I said.

"Almost." Drew shook his head. "One of the older riders, a *legendary* older rider, I should add, was cantering her horse with her friend. They came around a sharp corner and almost ran over the guy."

"Oh my God." I covered my mouth with my hand.

"Their horses swerved at the last second, apparently, and the guy didn't even know horses had been close until dirt clods flew back at him from the horses' hooves."

"Um, maybe we should run on the track instead," I said, only half joking. "Please make sure we go on a *human* trail."

"Promise," Drew said.

Fog surrounded us, making it feel as if there was no one else for miles. The moment felt like something out of a book.

I realized it was my turn to talk and I hadn't said a word. "Okay. Let's go—I'm trusting you here."

Drew bumped my shoulder with his. "You can trust me."

"Who *was* that rider?" I asked as I followed him into the woods. "The 'legendary' one?"

"Sasha Silver."

I sucked in a breath at her name. *Sasha Silver. Sasha Silver.* Her name rolled around in my brain as I followed Drew on autopilot as we entered the woods. We'd stepped onto a well-worn path. The dirt was marked with shoe imprints instead of horseshoes. Without a word, we started at a slow jog, side by side.

"Where did you go?" Drew asked. He had a soft smile on his face.

"What do you mean?"

"You're *here*, but you looked far away. Like you were thinking about something serious." Now our footsteps hit the dirt in tandem.

"Oh, I was just thinking." I paused midsentence. "You said 'Sasha Silver.' She and I are kind of connected in a way."

Drew motioned with his hand to the left side of the trail where it forked into two separate paths. We kept our jogging at a steady pace. When we really started to run, if we were doing it right, we wouldn't have the breath to talk.

"Don't tell me—she's your stepsister," Drew said.

I laughed. "No. But she and I both trained at Briar Creek Stables with the same instructor before we came to Canterwood. Her family still lives in Union, too, where my family is."

"Wow," Drew said, looking over at me. "Working with the same coach as Sasha is an incredible opportunity. Also a little scary and intimidating, I bet."

Drew *got* me. I don't know how, but he just did.

"You have no idea," I said. "You're the first one here to pick up on the scary part without me having to explain it first. Usually, I tell people that I trained at Briar Creek after Sasha and I get the 'Omigod, you were in the same stable as Sasha?! With her instructor? Did you see her?' and a zillion questions like that."

I adjusted my stride as my legs continued to warm up.

"I completely understand that," I continued. "Like you said, though, on the flipside I feel as though people are expecting me to be just like her. To be the next Briar-Creek-to-Canterwood-Crest prodigy."

"Do your parents make you feel that way?"

"Oh, not at all!" Thinking about them even for a second made my chest tighten. I missed them. "My parents are the best—they're not stage parents, and they don't want to micromanage my career. They were always there for me but never pushed me to compete."

Drew smiled. "They sound cool. I'm glad they didn't make you feel like you had to be Sasha two-point-oh when you came here."

"Not for a second. Mr. Conner hasn't either. I mean, I haven't even *seen* Sasha yet. The stable is always so busy. I'm not exactly looking for her, but I'd try to get enough courage to introduce myself if I ever see her."

"This is a small school," Drew said. "It doesn't feel that way, to me anyway, but you'll see Sasha sometime. When you do, I know you'll be *fine*—talk to her like the Lauren I'm chatting with now."

I smiled, knowing I was blushing. Hopefully, Drew would think it was because of the exercise.

Under the cover of trees, we were still shaded from direct sunlight. It came through in patches, lighting different spots of the trail, and had begun to burn off the fog.

"Thanks, Drew," I said. "If and when I do see Sasha, you'll be the first to know."

He grinned. "Good. Want to pick up the pace?"

I nodded. "I'm always ready."

12

A "FRIENDLY" LITTLE RACE

DREW MOVED FORWARD, FASTER. I MATCHED him, starting to feel endorphins kick in.

"At The Sweet Shoppe, you told me that you live with your dad," I said. "How is he about your riding?"

"Supportive all the way," Drew said. Sunlight glinted off his black hair as we ran through a less shaded stretch. "He was happy when I found riding. I'd been swimming and had tried a bunch of different sports, but I was missing *something*. He even tried sports with me—archery, indoor rock climbing, golf—everything."

"That's a good dad," I said, smiling.

"I think he was afraid that I wasn't totally happy because of my mom leaving. He cut back hours at work to be home more, made it clear that I could have friends over on the weekends, and did everything he could to compensate for my mom not being there."

"I know I said it before, but I'm sorry."

We were quiet for a few seconds. The only sound was the *whoosh* of our breaths, getting faster, and our shoes hitting the dirt.

"Thanks, Laur. I don't really talk about her much, but I don't know if I was missing a mom or if I just knew there was something else for me out there."

"How did you find riding?"

My question made Drew smile. "A coworker of my dad's invited us over for a barbecue. The guy and his wife had horses, and they asked if I wanted to ride. I didn't even hesitate. They saddled up a *really* old Appaloosa and explained the basics to me. The horse—Clark—was their daughter's old horse. She was in college, and she used to compete in Western classes on Clark."

"Oh, neat," I said. "Did you ride Western that day? I've never tried it—I really want to."

"Yeah, they put Western tack on Clark and led me to a small arena. I got on and everything just . . . *clicked*. I loved riding the second I sat in the saddle."

I grinned. "I love this story." It was a little harder to get words out—the faster jog was taking most of my breath.

"They let me ride Clark as long as I wanted. When I got in the car with my dad, I started to ask him if I could take lessons." Drew laughed. "But before I could ask, Dad told me he wanted to look into a nearby stable about lessons if I wanted to try riding. He said his coworker told him that he'd never seen anyone pick up riding so fast."

"That's so cool! Omigosh! And you said yes, of course, to the lessons, right?"

"I started the next weekend. Dad promised that I'd get my own horse if I still loved riding after a year."

"Enter Polo."

"My instructor helped me find him. I tried Polo and one other horse before I said I didn't need to ride any others. Polo was my guy."

"Aw, I love it." I brushed a bead of sweat off my forehead.

Drew checked his watch. "Want to really go for it? We're going to hit a straight lane really soon. It takes us out of the woods—my usual stopping point. We'll end up behind the cafeteria. I usually cool down by walking back to my dorm, or if I'm really hot, walking back and forth between my dorm hall and the caf."

"Let's go!"

Without waiting for him, I dug my shoes into the dirt and kicked into top gear.

"Towers!" Drew yelled. His shoes pounded the dirt, a few paces behind me.

I held back my laughter and focused on my breathing. Drew caught up, matching me stride for stride. Together, we ran.

And ran.

And ran.

Like we'd never run out of breath.

Like the path was never-ending.

Like we were feeding off each other's energy.

We ran until we broke an imaginary yellow finish-line ribbon in a dead heat. If it had been a track meet, judges wouldn't be able to determine a winner. Even with playback.

I bent over, hands on my knees, gasping. That's what not running consistently did to me! My breaths were ragged, and I gulped air. Beside me, Drew grabbed the hem of his T-shirt and lifted it up to his face. He wiped sweat from his forehead.

I tried not to stare as he exposed flat abs. He had the lean body of a swimmer combined with the strong, muscular body of a rider. I blushed, looking away as my breathing started to slow. I reached down, grabbing one ankle, holding the position, then switching.

The fog had disappeared—I hadn't even noticed

when it had completely lifted—and sunlight, strong for October, illuminated the campus, which had been dim when I'd last seen it. Running through the woods had felt like time had skipped ahead.

"What did you think?" Drew asked as we started walking side by side.

"That was *awesome*," I said. "I love that trail. It's the perfect length, and the shade is definitely welcome for this time of year."

"I'm really glad you liked it. It's my favorite outdoor running path."

"I—I had a lot of fun running with you," I said. I looked at him, and he locked his eyes on mine. It almost made me forget what I was going to say. "Thanks for showing me the path and for going with me. You got me out of my head for a while, and I *really* needed that."

Drew grinned. "Even though you cheated at the end—"

I gasped. "I would never!"

"Even despite *that*," Drew continued, laughing, "I had a lot of fun too. I feel great and ready to tackle the day. You said you're used to running alone, but if you ever want to run together again, count me in."

"I'd love that. Maybe we can run together, like, three or four mornings a week before class?"

Getting to do this again with Drew would *definitely* make it easy for me to get out of bed so early.

"Sounds great."

Drew and I smiled at each other. I couldn't wait to tell Khloe! Maybe it was the endorphins from exercise, or getting to spend time with Drew before classes, but I was giddy.

We chatted about our day as we cooled down, and Drew walked me to Hawthorne before heading back to Blackwell.

Best. Early. Morning. Yet.

13

COSTUME CONFESSION

BACK IN MY ROOM, KHLOE WAS IN THE SHOWER.

I knocked and cracked open the bathroom door. Steam poured out with a wave of Khloe's strawberry body wash.

"Mooorning!" I sang.

Khloe stuck her head out of the shower curtain. "Someone's happy this morning." She peered at me, then grinned. "Your run with Drew was awful, wasn't it?"

I nodded. "Horrible. When you get out of the shower, I'll tell you all about it."

Khloe made a pretend-sad face. "I'm sorry. I'll be out in five, and then you can tell your roomie all about it. I'll do my very best to make you feel better." She winked at me and disappeared back behind the curtain.

Smiling, I closed the bathroom door and slipped out

of my sweaty clothes. I tossed them in my overflowing hamper. Laundry was on my to-do list this weekend. I put on my terry-cloth white robe with multicolored polka dots and sat at my desk.

I opened my laptop and pulled up my blog. I clicked "new post" and started typing. My fingers flew over the keys, and just as Khloe turned off the water, I was proofreading my post.

Lauren Towers's Blog

7:02 a.m.: Life is good!

I don't have much time to write this morning, but I feel like I'm going to burst if I don't!!! I already blogged about one thing in my last post, but I've had time to reflect on it, and I have a few more thoughts. The second awesome-slash-amazing thing just happened. ☺

About the show: I blogged last time that Whisper and I attended the schooling show hosted by Canterwood. It was our first show together, which on its own is something that makes me *très, très* proud.

As I've said a bunch of times, the schooling show was the first competition since Red Oak. The show that wouldn't let go until I competed again. I couldn't have been happier with the results of the schooling show.

Whisper is *incredibly* green and new to the show circuit compared to most of the other horses we were up against. She's only five, and we've been a pair since summer. I would have been truly happy if we'd attended the show, gotten Whisper the experience and feel of a competition, and not won any ribbons.

It would have also been enough for me to show and not place. I had *everything* to prove. Not to anyone else, either. To myself. I needed to get back in the arena at a competitive level and prove it to myself that I could do it. I wasn't trying to make myself do something that I didn't want to do—I'd been excited about the show since Mr. C had announced it.

Excited and terrified.

Getting back into the competitive circle, though, was my ultimate reason for joining Canterwood's riding team. This schooling show was the *parfait* (Oops, right. Promised KK that I'd translate all French words on my blog! Will do starting here.) opportunity for me as an equestrian. I didn't have to travel, worry about how that would affect Whisper, and get the both of us used to new riding spaces. Obviously, we can't always show on home turf, but it was exactly what Whisper and I needed for our first competition. Next time, we'll be ready to take the next step and travel.

Okay, so (I need to get to the point!) completing two classes with Whisper and being more than happy with our rides would have felt like a huge win to me even if we hadn't placed.

Except, as I blogged last time, we actually DID win a class. The show closed with a blue and a red ribbon for Whisper and me.

I'm staring at them now, and I still can't believe they're mine. Sorry for rambling! Geeze! All I really wanted to say was that I'm still thinking about the show and how grateful I am to have a wonderful, willing, smart, beautiful horse like Whisper. I cannot wait for Mr. C to announce our next competition.

So, the NEW thing: I just got back to my room after my first run with D. ☺ ☺ ☺ ☺ (I could do a row of smiley faces! LOL!)

The weather was perfect, and it was foggy, which made it even better—like D and I were the only students on campus. We talked while we warmed up, and I learned more abt D. I can't learn enough. I always want to know more and more and more!

I was nervous that he wouldn't want to run with me again. But at the end, I actually asked if he wanted to run with me again. And not just, "Let's run again sometime," but "Let's run three or four mornings a week." He said YES! *Ooh la la!*

Yes! KK's out of the shower, and now I get to tell her all about my morning.

Posted by Lauren Towers

After I'd told Khloe all about my morning run, I also told her a secret that I'd been keeping to myself.

"Omigod," Khloe said. "Please, please don't tell me that you really hate TV and you've pretended this whole time!"

I shook my head, pulling a plastic box from the top of my closet. "Every October, I usually wear a Halloween-themed shirt every day. Every. Day."

Khloe looked into the box. "This isn't at all what I was afraid you'd say."

"It's almost mid-October, and I haven't followed my tradition. I was afraid Canterwood wasn't the place to wear a shirt with a witch one day and a ghost the next. But I really, really miss my shirts and wanted your opinion."

"Laur! I wish you'd come to me sooner. No one cares if you wear a Halloween shirt during *Christmas*. Wear whatever you want—whatever makes you happy!" Khloe looked through the shirts. "From what I've seen, you've got an awesome collection. Start wearing them!"

I slid into a gray tee with a scary black tree faded in the background. *Now* it was starting to feel like Halloween around here.

14

SPACED ON STUDYING

I DASHED TO THE STABLE ON FRIDAY AFTERnoon. Giant, dark clouds gathered overhead and I clutched my umbrella—I'd learned my lesson from last time. I hoped it waited to storm until I was back in my room. I'd pull the curtains aside and curl up on my bed with a book or magazine. Truly a *très parfait* way to end the week.

Now I couldn't wait for today's lesson. Mr. Conner had told us yesterday that we'd be working inside on dressage. I'd be the first one in the arena—I'd been waiting for this all day.

"Laur!"

I stopped, mid-jog, and turned.

Khloe hurried up the sidewalk toward me. She was dressed in casual Friday clothes—a new policy that

Mr. Conner had extended for the advanced team. Khloe had paired a graphic T-shirt—off-white with an orange can of Slice and ragged hems—with fawn breeches and paddock boots. A small blue tote bag with a purple sequin heart was over her arm.

"Thanks for waiting," she said.

"Um, of course. I would have waited for you in our room if you'd told me you would only be a few minutes. And totally crushing on your bag, FYI."

Khloe tugged an orange elastic off her wrist, braiding her hair as we walked. "Thanks! It was in my mail pile—Mom sent it. Anyway, I thought I'd stay a while to study, but I decided to bring my book and study in Ever's stall."

I held up a hand. "Stop. Right. There. Khloe Kinsella, what could possibly be important enough to study on a Friday before lessons? *Science? History?*"

Khloe rolled her eyes. "Puh-lease, LT. As if I'd stay inside, skipping extra time with my lovely, amaze friends and dream horse to study for *school*."

She opened her bag and dug out a book, handing it to me. "I forgot to study my horse manual. Oops. At least I've got until the end of your lesson to read."

Panic raced through me, and my palms instantly started sweating.

I hadn't studied for today.

I visualized my horse manual and knew exactly where it was—on the top shelf of my desk, with a green sticky note at the beginning of the pages that I needed to read. Last night I'd looked through the chapter, and it had been something I knew very little about—different types of worms and parasites. The color photo of some kind of creepy-crawly bug had made me shudder and shut the book, vowing to study before I went to sleep.

This afternoon, when I'd gone back to my room to change, I'd breezed right by the book. If I'd seen the red cover, it would have reminded me that I'd spent all of the previous night on schoolwork. No equine study.

"You okay?" Khloe asked. "You look like you've seen a ghost. Halloween's still a couple of weeks away. . . ."

"I wish I'd seen a ghost," I said. "Instead I'm about to see Mr. Conner turned Incredible Hulk."

Khloe's light brown brows arched. "What? Why?"

I handed Khloe back her book. "I didn't study my horse manual. At all. Totally spaced."

Khloe put her book away, linking her arm through mine as we walked. "There's no guarantee that you'll have a quiz today. It's Friday, so maybe Mr. Conner will save it for Monday."

"I hate gambling like that," I said. "Plus, skipping reading keeps putting me more and more behind." I groaned, slapping a palm to my forehead. "I'm so dumb. I can't believe I did that."

"Laur, don't say that about yourself." Khloe's tone was low and serious. "I'm not cool with you putting yourself down in front of me. What if you find someone who's already studied and brought their book? Borrow the book, study until you have to be in the arena for warm-up."

"I have to groom and tack up," I said.

"Let me take care of Whisper. I'll have her ready and waiting for you."

I squeezed Khloe's arm. "You are the best. I don't even know what to say—thank you. But I can't let you do that. You already planned to spend your time studying— you forgot too. I can't let you get in trouble because I messed up."

Khloe waved her free hand. "I'll study during your lesson after I groom and tack up. Plenty of time."

I smiled. "It's not and you know it. I'm just going to have to risk it and see if he quizzes us or not. But I really, really can't thank you enough for your offer."

"Okay," Khloe said. "I understand and I won't keep asking. But I *will* be crossing my fingers that Mr. C doesn't quiz your class. Especially since it's a dressage lesson and it's all you've been talking about since last night."

We reached the stable and stepped inside though the giant front doors, which had been slid open. The back door was open too, and a gentle breeze blew through the stable. The horses seemed to enjoy the fresh air—most of them had their heads poked over stall doors. Some slept while others watched the frenzy of riders around them.

"Good luck reading, and I'll see you later," I said, letting go of Khloe's arm.

"Okay. I'll be channeling the part of me that I'm, like, *certain* has ESP and will be telling Mr. Conner, 'Don't quiz the seventh-grade intermediate team today,' until your lesson."

I smiled like only Khloe could make me smile. "Thanks, KK."

"If it works, you have to agree to be interviewed by the magazines and newspapers that will want a witness of my skill. 'Kay?"

"I'll give a dozen interviews for you," I promised. "Maybe I'll become your publicity person or your manager."

Khloe tapped her temple. "Now you're thinking!"

Laughing, we waved and split. I took a left, heading

down the side aisle to the tack room, and Khloe went straight down the main aisle toward Ever's stall.

As I gathered Whisper's tack, I pictured Khloe sitting in Ever's stall and channeling her ESP. The image made me feel a little better. Not that I thought she'd be able to reach Mr. Conner, but Khlo was thinking about me.

I rushed through Whisper's grooming and tacking up. I wanted to get in the arena and be with my friends. Being alone was driving me crazy. Plus, I wanted time to pass faster so I'd just *know*.

"Sorry! Oh, I'm so sorry!" I apologized to Whisper when she squealed and whipped her tail from side to side. I'd tightened her girth too fast and had pinched her skin. "Sweetie, I am so, so sorry. You didn't deserve that." I loosened her girth and carefully retightened it.

I moved up to Whisper's cheek and stroked it. She kept her head high, ears back a little. I kept petting her. "You know I'd never mean to hurt you, right? I love you so much, and I shouldn't have been rushing. Not when it comes to stuff related to you. I can rush *my* stuff—not yours."

Whisper's head lowered, slowly, until her muzzle rested in my hand. I scratched between her ears and she closed her eyes, letting my fingers get any itches.

"Forgive me?" I asked.

Whisper opened her eyes, her curly, long lashes winking at me. Her beautiful, liquid brown eyes were full of expression—I truly believed I could understand some of her thoughts from looking into her eyes.

Her ears swiveled forward, and she bumped my arm with her muzzle. Her whiskers tickled me.

I grinned. "I'll take that as a yes." I put my arms around her neck, and she let me rest on her. Hugging her and inhaling her sweet scent of fresh hay and cinnamon treats calmed my anxiety. My thudding heartbeat slowed, and I took a deep breath.

"Hopefully, we'll doing a twenty-meter circle in a little while," I said. "Otherwise . . ." I shook my head. I didn't want to think of the alternative.

I picked up Whisper's bridle from across the stall door and slid the reins over her head. Whisper took the bit and looked like a stone statue as I buckled the straps and put on my helmet.

I grasped the reins under her chin, taking a firm hold. Whisper had been better about not rushing out of the stall, and Mike and Doug had reported the same, and I wanted to keep it that way. I left the stall first, and Whisper followed at an easy walk. Once we were in the aisle, I let her walk beside me to the indoor arena.

We were the first ones here. Part of the arena had dressage markers ready for our class. Seeing the markers made me shiver with excitement. I *had* to do dressage today! I mounted and let Whisper walk on a loose rein to the arena wall. *Even if we do have a quiz, I've been reading about horses forever,* I reminded myself. *Maybe I won't get every question right, but I surely know enough to pass the quiz.*

Soon Lexa, Drew, Cole, and Clare joined me for our warm-up. I trotted Whisper up to Lexa and Clare, who were talking.

". . . definitely a party must," Clare said to Lexa, then looked over and saw me.

"Lauren! Sneak!" Clare said, shaking her head.

I made a *who me I'm innocent* face. "I didn't know you two were talking about a *party*. What party?"

Lexa mock-scowled at me. "I think you know quite enough." She looked at Clare. "We have to tighten security. LT's getting too much info."

"Agreed. No more breaches," Clare said.

"I wasn't coming over to bribe you two about my party details," I said. "I just wanted to say hi."

"Uh-huh," Lexa said, looking at me sideways.

The three of us burst into giggles.

"No, really," I said. "Do you guys think we'll have a quiz today?"

"I don't know," Clare said. "We didn't have one yesterday, so maybe."

That made my heart sink a little.

"But it's also Friday," Lexa said, patting Honor's neck. "Mr. Conner might just let us go straight to lessons."

"You study?" Clare asked.

I shook my head, my hands starting to sweat again. Whisper's reins were slippery in my hands.

"I skimmed it," Lexa said. "Clare?"

"I didn't have much homework yesterday, so I did read the chapter. I can give you the highlights—maybe that'll help, Laur," Clare said.

"Please! I owe you. Big-time."

Clare put her reins in one hand and let Fuego walk at a relaxed pace. "Okay, so the chapter was all about worms and parasites. Mostly about how to identify a worm if found in a horse's manure, when to consider whether or not your horse might have a parasite, and the signs of the most common ones." She took a breath. "Um, also how horses contract these and how to cure and prevent the most common types."

"What's a common worm?" I asked.

"Flatworm," Clare said. "If a horse has them, they're found in manure. They look like—"

"Please bring your horses to the center." Mr. Conner's voice stopped Clare midsentence.

"Sorry," she whispered.

I shook my head. "No way. Thank you for offering and trying. I really appreciate it."

Lexa, Clare, and I rode our horses over to Mr. Conner. We stopped them in front of him. Cole and Drew joined at the end of our line. I scanned Mr. Conner—trying to find *some* indication about whether or not we'd be quizzed. His clipboard didn't look like it had any extra papers, and he didn't have any folders. Nothing suggested a quiz.

"I hope you've all had a good Friday," Mr. Conner said. "As you know, today we'll be working on dressage. Markers have been erected, and you'll be taking turns executing different moves."

Yes! No quiz! I let out the breath I'd been holding since I'd met up with Khloe. She was going to freak when I told her and attribute this to her ESP.

"Before we begin dressage, I need you to dismount and come take this from me," Mr. Conner said. I watched and as if in slow motion, he held up five papers with pens clipped to them. "This is a short quiz covering last night's chapter," he continued. "If you read the material, you should have no problem."

And if you didn't, you are going to flunk.

We dismounted, and my knees felt wobbly when I landed on the ground. Mr. Conner handed each of us the quiz and pen.

"Spread out a little and answer the questions," Mr. Conner said. "You've got ten minutes."

I felt hot as I led Whisper over to a space along the arena wall. I put the paper on the ledge and looped Whisper's reins over my arm.

Five questions.

Fill in the blank.

No true or false.

No shade the correct bubble.

With only five questions, there was room to miss only one question.

Stop and focus! I scribbled my name at the top and looked at the first question.

I. List at least two types of worms that are common in horses.

Flatworms and

I stopped. I *knew* this. It didn't come from the book. One of my stable horses had been in infected with . . . *think! Think!*

Got it!

I added *roundworms* in the first blank. Question one down.

2. Describe two ways horses can become infected with flatworms.

My pen hovered.

And hovered.

Move on to the next question!

But I didn't know the answer to number three.

Or four.

Or five.

Sweat trickled down my back as I stared at the questions as if they'd somehow change to questions that I could answer.

"Time!" Mr. Conner called. "Please bring me your quizzes."

I shuffled my feet in the dirt, knowing my face had to be eight different shades of red, and handed my paper to Mr. Conner. I turned away fast before I could see the look on his face. We lined up, standing beside our horses, and looked at him.

"Please give me a few moments to look through these, dismiss anyone who did not pass, and then, for those who did, we'll go over the answers and I'll answer any questions you may have."

I kept my head down, not able to look at Mr. Conner or anyone else. My stomach was upset, and it seemed as though it was taking *hours* for Mr. Conner to go through our papers.

"All right," Mr. Conner said. "Thank you all for completing the quizzes."

I braced myself.

"Lauren, please leave the arena," Mr. Conner said. "I'll see you at class on Monday."

I was the only one.

I nodded, unable to speak.

Embarrassment burned my body as I left the lineup and walked Whisper past Mr. Conner. I kept my eyes down, feeling like everyone was staring at my back. The arena exit was impossibly far away, but the second Whisper and I were through, I burst into tears.

15

TODAY KEEPS GETTING BETTER. NOT!

RAIN SLAMMED AGAINST MY DORM ROOM windows. I'd made it back to my room before the downpour after I'd untacked Whisper and left the stable. I was on my stomach on my bed, reading all of the pages I'd missed in my horse manual.

The bathroom door opened, and steam followed Khloe out. A brown towel was wrapped around her hair, and she'd pulled on blue-and-green-striped cotton pants and a matching T-shirt. Khloe gave me a tiny smile, her eyes falling on my book. She'd just gotten back from her lesson and hopped in the shower.

"How's the reading?" Khloe asked.

I slid in my bookmark and closed the book. "I caught up on all of the past chapters and took notes. Just got to today's chapter, but I'm going to break and read it later this weekend."

"Good plan. You read a lot, too." Khloe pulled the towel turban off her head and shook out her blond hair. She sprayed Bumble and bumble Prep through her locks and used a wide-toothed comb to detangle any knots.

"I wouldn't have had a lot of reading if I'd kept up with it in the first place," I said. "Today was totally my fault, and I learned my lesson—believe me."

I got up, grabbed my assignment calendar off my desk, and walked over to Khloe, who sat cross-legged on her bed.

"See?" I pointed to each day's assignment block for the next week. "I've got it on my calendar to read for riding. If it's in here, it's as good as done."

Khloe smiled, peering at the calendar. "I'll have to use you to keep me on track. Especially since we learned that my ESP needs some fine-tuning."

"Should I add that to my calendar?" I teased.

Khloe's phone buzzed. She leaned over and checked the screen on her BlackBerry.

"Zack," she said, grinning. "He wants to know if I'm busy tomorrow night!"

"You're going on another daaate! You know what that means . . . spa day tomorrow."

Khloe's fingers moved furiously over her keypad, and then she looked up at me. "Spa day sounds perfect."

"I'll make a list of what we can do so we don't forget anything. Especially since we got some new products since last time."

I went back to my desk, found a pink notebook with light purple paper inside, and took it to my bed. I glanced at Khloe—she was lost in Zack Land. Smiling to myself, I opened the notebook. On a clean page, I started writing.

♥ *Khloe & Lauren's Spa Day:*

Pedicure

Use tea tree oil and mint scrub, metal foot files,
foot polisher, lotion

Remove old polish

Prep nails for painting: trim cuticles, clean under
nails, trim nails, file, buff, apply coat of base

Paint toenails

I read over my pedicure section, double-checking to make sure I'd included everything.

My phone chimed, signaling a new e-mail. I opened my mail. It was a comment on my latest blog post from "Anonymous." My stomach dropped when I read the message.

16

ANONYMOUS =
ANNOYING

Anonymous: I'm clapping for you too, since it seems like that's what all of your friends are doing. Congrats on winning a class in an intermediate schooling show. Come on. How many times are you going to blog about that?! You should be embarrassed instead. I mean, you went from the A circuit to schooling shows. You must have hit your head REALLY hard when you fell at Red Oak. There's no other reason why you'd be this excited about getting first and second at such a low-level show. Get a brain scan to be safe. . . .

"Are you kidding me?" I asked aloud.

I deleted the message and put my phone back on

my nightstand. I opened my computer and logged in to my blog.

I hovered above the blog comment, ready to delete it with a click.

"You okay?" Khloe asked.

"Some jerk just left a nasty comment on my blog." I rolled my eyes.

"What? Let me see! I'll hunt them down." Khloe was up and sitting next to me in seconds. She scanned my laptop screen.

"I'm just going to delete it and not reply," I said. "I guess I should lock my blog from now on."

"No, don't do that," Khloe said. "Think about it. If you delete the comment, 'Anonymous' will think he or she got to you. That'll be like letting Anonymous win."

I moved my mouse pointer away from the delete button, but still wasn't convinced.

"So I just do nothing?"

"Not a thing. Don't lock your blog. Or respond to the comment. Or change what you blog about. If you act like this was just any other comment, then Anonymous will get *really* annoyed. I doubt he or she will leave another comment, but if that happens, you have to keep up the same protocol."

I nodded, understanding where Khloe was coming from. "I get it now. I can do that."

"I'm sorry you're dealing with an idiot like this," Khloe said, frowning. "Try to stick it out unless the comments turn supernasty. Or if you feel like you're being bullied. Promise you'll tell me if you get another comment, okay?"

"Promise," I said, logging out of my blog. "So, did you make plans with Zack?"

Khloe grinned. "Chinese food and a movie tomorrow night."

I high-fived her. "Yay!"

"Tomorrow's going to be awesome. Spa day and a date with Zack."

I started to reply when my Skype line rang. "It's Brielle!"

"Have fun!" Khloe said. "I've got a stack of *Celeb Dish* mags waiting." She went back to her bed, and I answered Brielle's call.

"Hi!" I said, waving when Brielle's image popped into view. Her pale, creamy skin stood out against her black hair. It hung in soft waves—a new look for Bri. Ana and I used to joke that Bri's flatiron was on more than it was off. For Christmas one year, we'd even gotten her a mini portable one that took batteries, so she could straighten on the go.

"Lauren! Look who else is here." Brielle moved her chair over, and Ana waved at me with both hands.

"Hey, LT!" Ana said, grinning.

"A! You cut your hair! Wow, it looks amazing!" I stared at Ana's light-brown hair. The last time I'd seen Ana, her hair had been just past her shoulders, with blond highlights we'd *begged* her mom to let Ana get. Now her locks were cut into a textured bob and shaped with pomade. The highlights were gone.

Ana touched her hair. "Oh, I totally forgot that you haven't seen it. It feels like I chopped it off forever ago."

"You," I said, pointing a finger at Ana, "refused to ever cut your hair that short. Even when I swore it would look great. What made you go for it?"

"That would be me," Brielle said, raising a hand. She and Ana glanced at each other, then burst into laughter.

I blinked, waiting for them to fill me in. They kept giggling.

"I want in on the joke," I said. I kept the slight hurt that I felt out of my voice. *Be realistic, Lauren,* I told myself. *Of course Bri and Ana are going to have their own stuff. You have the same thing with Khlo and Lex.*

"I promised," Brielle said, between giggles, "that if Ana hated her haircut, I would let her shave my head."

Ana turned sideways, facing Bri. "And I *so* didn't believe you. At all."

"So I actually bought hair clippers from Ulta to prove it," Bri said, starting to laugh again. "But thank God that Ana loved her hair. "Or I'd look . . . well, not like the girl that Will fell for when we first started dating."

"You mixed it up too," I said. "Loving the waves."

I fought the urge to touch my own hair. Nothing had changed since the last time I'd seen my friends. It was still long, brown, and wavy. No new styles or cuts.

"Really? Thanks!" Brielle grinned into the webcam. "Ana taught me, and even though it adds, like, twenty extra minutes to my beauty routine in the morning, it's *so* worth it."

I sniffed, pretending to hold back tears. "It's like I don't even know either of you anymore!"

"Eh," Ana said, waving a hand at me. "We're still the same girls, at the same school, dating the same, um, guys. Dating the same guys! Yep!" Ana spun Bri's desk chair around in a circle.

"You should be *so* glad you're not here right now," Bri said to me. "Ana's having a spaz attack."

Bri glanced over at Ana, ready to kick off into another circle, and shot her a look. Brielle leaned over so her face was off camera, and Ana was left onscreen. Brielle must have mouthed something or given Ana a famous *you don't want to mess with me right now* look. Ana toyed with the ends of her hair, and the chair was still. Ana smiled at me, and Brielle appeared back onscreen.

"Really, Laur, you're not missing anything," Bri added. Her eyes weren't looking into the camera. It looked like she was staring at her keyboard. "Nothing but the same."

"Not *everything* can be the same. What about two very cute boyfriends? How are Will and Jeremy?"

Silence.

I'd expected Bri and Ana to talk over each other to tell me about their guys.

"Laur?" Bri asked, peering at me. "We lost the connection for a second. Can you see and hear us?"

"Loud and clear," I said. "I didn't even know we'd gotten cut off."

"Oh, no worries," Brielle said. "Ana and I are dying to hear about *your* guy! Tell us everything about Drew!"

I started to say they'd missed my question and I wanted to hear about their boyfriends, but I couldn't pass up any opportunity to talk about Drew.

"Get comfy," I said. "You're going to be sorry that you asked."

17
THE SMURF AND THE
MUD-SOAKED

"YOU LOOK LIKE A SMURF," KHLOE SAID, giggling.

Standing next to her in our bathroom, I peered at my reflection. My face was a brilliant shade of blue. We were deep in spa Saturday.

"And you look like you lost in a mud fight," I teased back.

"We've got to get a pic of this," Khloe said.

Khloe pulled her BlackBerry from the pocket of her terry-cloth robe.

"Most definitely," I said. "You have to tag me when you upload it to FaceSpace." I looked at her and grinned. "You should *so* use the photo as your new head shot. You look *très* glam."

"Ha, ha. Pose!"

Khloe threw her arm around me, and we tilted our heads toward each other. The flash went off, and Khloe turned the phone so we could both see the screen. We looked so silly—giant grins, painted faces, and skinny neon Goody headbands to keep stray hair out of the mask.

"Love," I said. "We should forgo makeup from now on and go to classes like this."

Khloe brought the phone closer to her eyes, squinting at the screen. "You know, if I cropped you out—"

"Hey!"

"No, I can't do that, we're too close together." Khloe kept talking as if she hadn't heard me. "Maybe you should take a photo of me like this with my good camera. What if I sent it with my real head shot to casting directors?"

"Well . . . um, what are you going for, exactly?" I asked, sitting on the edge of the bathtub.

Khloe adjusted her blue headband. "The pic would show my silly side! Casting directors would see that I'm not afraid to be silly. I'd be the *perf* actor for a role on CTV Family Network."

"Any particular show in mind?"

She turned around, hopping up to sit on the edge of the sink, and looked at me. "It would all start with a guest spot," Khloe said, talking faster and faster. "*Unconventional* would be the ONE. I could play a cousin from L.A. who comes to visit Taryn's family in Alabama. I'd be all L.A. glam. Since Taryn's fam is hippie and like, only eats food they grow, I would be the girl out of her element."

Khloe bowed her head and looked up at me with a smile.

"*Unconventional* is an awesome show," I said. "You'd be an amazing addition to the cast. You should send your résumé, reel, and head shot."

I touched my face. "Time to rinse!" I motioned for Khloe to get off the sink and turned on the water. Maybe if I didn't bring up the mud-mask photo and distracted her with our next activity—manis . . . I turned on the water and bent over the sink.

Blue water swirled down the drain as I rinsed. I patted my face dry with an espresso-colored towel.

"Here you go!" Khloe chirped. She thrust her Nikon at me. "Snap away!"

My mouth open and closed.

"I didn't even hear you leave the bathroom," I said. I had to tell Khloe my opinion. Maybe I was wrong and a casting director would adore the photo. But my gut said it was better to stay professional. "Khlo, about the picture. I'm not exactly sure—"

Khloe's brown eyes settled on my face. Then she burst into laughter.

What?

"I wondered how long it was going to take you!" Khloe said. She put the camera on a stack of bath towels. "I was totally messing with you, LT."

"Khloeee!" I swatted her arm.

"There's *nooo* way the photo of us will go anywhere but FaceSpace. It would be career suicide if I sent in a photo that looked like, as I think you put it so sweetly earlier, I 'lost in a mud fight.'"

We laughed.

"The image of your face covered in the mask would be copied and e-mailed to every casting director from Los Angeles to New York City," I said, pretend-serious.

A solemn Khloe nodded. "They'd look at my other head shots and just see 'Mud Girl.'"

"You'd have to stop acting immediately."

Khloe's eyes widened, and the super-dry mask on her forehead cracked. "A bored assistant would swipe the photo because it made her laugh. At a party one Saturday night, her New York studio apartment would be packed, and everyone would take a picture of *my* photo."

"Mud Girl would go from phone to phone. E-mail to

e-mail. People would recognize you on the street."

I bit the inside of my cheek to keep from giggling. Khloe could turn *anything* into an acting exercise.

"I'd have to move to a tiny, remote village in Switzerland." Khloe shook her head, her expression downcast.

"I would come with you," I said. "You never leave a best friend behind. Plus, you'd need someone to help you with recovery after surgery."

"Oh, right. Since e-mail goes everywhere, I'd have to get a nose job and pump up my lips with whatever they use. I'd change my name, get colored contacts, and dye my hair."

And Khloe and I continued to tell the saga of Mud Girl well into our manicures.

18

NO-FAIL ZONE

I SETTLED INTO THE SADDLE FOR TUESDAY'S lesson. I'd read every page in our horse manual—*twice*—in case Mr. Conner tested us.

After Friday's failed quiz, Mr. Conner had called me into his office on Monday. While my teammates had warmed up their horses, I'd answered different questions about worms and parasites. My studying had paid off. I'd gotten each question right, and Mr. Conner shooed me out of his office to tack up and get in the arena.

I walked Whisper toward the big window. The Halloween window clings that had gone up yesterday made me smile and get that *feeling*. I couldn't even describe it, but I only felt this way around Halloween. I loved it more than my birthday! I had a dozen Halloween T-shirts and long-sleeved shirts that I wore during October.

The stable had decorations everywhere. But it wasn't just the stable. I'd left my room this afternoon and, on my rush to the stable, spotted decorations in Hawthorne, in the classrooms, caf, and all over the outside of campus.

The second I had free time, I was going to walk the campus and look at each and every decoration. I'd probably even take pictures for Chatter or FaceSpace. I shook my head. It made me think of New York City tourists who stopped, took pictures, and almost got run over by taxis as they gawked at famous buildings or popular restaurants. *You're going to look just like that,* I thought, giggling to myself. *At least there aren't any cabs or bicyclists to worry about.*

Whisper and I passed the window. Smiling ghosts, pumpkins making silly faces, black cats, and a grinning green-faced witch had been scattered over the glass. I knew I'd stare at them every day until Halloween was over. "Look, girl, aren't the decorations fun? It's our first Halloween together."

"Someone's getting excited." A smiling Lexa rode next to me. "You haven't moved from the window for about, oh, five solid minutes."

"Guilty. You haven't seen anything yet. I actually considered skipping this lesson to walk around campus to see the decorations." I gave Lex an innocent smile.

"Oh, LT. You've got it bad. Everyone has their favorite holiday, though. I mean, when my family goes to New York City every few Christmases I practically walk from the Upper East Side to the Lower East Side to see the holiday transformation."

We let our horses walk, and the two mares kept an easy pace. Lexa and I were still the only two here yet.

"I love New York during Christmas. My sister and I walked along Fifth Avenue once and looked at the window displays. They're *très belle!*" I giggled. "Becca and I wouldn't go in any of the stores because they were so expensive—we were afraid the manager wouldn't even let us in."

Lexa laughed. "Oh, right! Those designer stores are intimidating. I go to Macy's. Best displays ever. Plus, I can actually afford some of the clothes."

"Speaking of clothes, I told Khloe about my Halloween wardrobe. Did you notice that I'm wearing Halloween-themed shirts all of a sudden?"

Lexa raised an eyebrow. "I did. But I didn't know it was a thing. What's a 'Halloween wardrobe'?"

I looked up when Cole and Clare entered the arena. Lexa and I waved as they started warming up their horses at the opposite end of the arena.

"There's *one* store that has the best Halloween tees and long-sleeved shirts on the planet: Target. Every year, I go there and buy new Halloween shirts. They're *insanely* inexpensive, and in August I start saving my allowance so I can get a lot of them. Some of the tees are, like, five dollars!"

Lexa motioned that we turn the horses and began a circle in the opposite direction. Whisper was a little tight on the turn; her not-fully warmed muscles made her circle sloppy. The change of direction would stretch her out.

"Sweet deal," Lexa said. "I'm going to start shopping there! So . . . ." She looked at me expectantly. "How many tees are in this 'Halloween wardrobe'?"

I smoothed Whisper's mane so that I didn't have to look at Lexa. If I did, she would *know*. "Oh," I said. "Like ten, maybe?"

Lexa snorted. "Lauren Towers."

I looked at her. "What?" My tone was hiiigh—like I'd just sucked helium from a balloon.

"Do I have to ask you the question again and again until you tell me the truth?"

"How—how—," I sputtered. "You always know when I'm lying! Not fair!"

Lexa grinned, leaning over to pat my shoulder. "Oh, sweetie, it doesn't help when your face turns red, you won't look me in the eye, and your voice gets several octaves higher than usual."

"I'm going to make Khloe teach me how to lie," I said, pretend-grumbling. "She has to have learned that in acting class."

Lexa didn't say a word. She just stared. Waiting. Waiting for me to spill.

"Okay, okay. So I *might* be a little obsessed," I said. "I brought about ten of my favorite Halloween shirts to Canterwood. But I have at least twenty more in my closet at home."

"I love it," Lexa said. She smiled, shaking her head. "Learning new things about friends—especially stuff that not *everyone* knows—makes me feel like there's a tighter bond."

Honor bobbed her head as if agreeing with her owner.

"I agree. Completely. With that in mind, here's something that everyone at school can see, but no one's ever asked me about it. Only Ana and Brielle, my best friends at Yates."

I pressed my boot against Whisper's side, giving her continuous gentle pressure. She responded exactly as I'd hoped, sidestepping toward Honor. Lexa's eyes scanned my face, her own full of curiosity.

"Every year," I started, "I wear a Halloween shirt from October first until the end of the month. If I don't wear a Halloween-themed shirt to school, I sleep in one. Then, after the month's over, I pack them away until next year."

I cringed, closing an eye and peeking at Lex through the other. "Was that too weird for you? Are you going to drop me and become BFFs with Delia?"

"Please. Don't dis Delia," Lexa said, grinning. "Every time she gets in trouble for talking on her cell in the hallways, texting during class, IMing at lunch—she always gets teary and says she forgot the rule." She frowned. "But somehow, she's *still* getting away with it, and this is her second year at Canterwood. I think I'll keep you and not get between Delia and her iPhone best friend."

We giggled.

"I like sharing stuff with you. I'm glad you don't think I'm weird."

Out of the corner of my eye, I saw Drew lead Polo into the arena and adjust his left stirrup leather.

"Everyone has something like that," Lex said. "I don't think you're weird at all. Maybe after our lesson I can come over and you can show me the shirts you brought."

"I'd love to."

"Cool! Want to trot the horses around the arena wall?"

With a nod from me, we asked our horses for a faster pace. We were halfway across the arena before something hit me.

"Hey," I said to Lex. "What's *your* thing?"

Lexa got a teasing grin on her face. "I'll tell you. Someday!"

"Lexaaa!"

She cued Honor to canter, kicking up dirt behind them. She laughed as Honor dashed away from Whisper and me.

"Oh, not happening! You're not getting away that easy!"

I let out the reins, and Whisper and I charged after Honor, chasing her across the arena. I barely noticed that Clare, Cole, and Drew had stopped their horses and were watching us, laughing.

"C'mon, guys!" I called, motioning to them. "It's reverse tag and Lexa's *it*!"

Within seconds, we were all laughing and engaged in tag. The game melted away the stress of the day, and everyone was having fun. Cole let out a whoop when he tagged Lexa.

"Drew's it!" Cole said.

My eyes centered on Drew. I was determined to be the one to tag him.

Showered and sitting at my desk, I picked up my phone. There was thing I had to do before I started homework.

I opened BlackBerry Messenger.

Lauren:

I had a lot of fun playing tag! I hope you don't feel bad that I tagged you. Twice. ☺

I sent the message to Drew, put my phone on my desk, and started pulling books from my bag. I was going to be up a *long* time tonight. Teachers had announced that midterms were next month—right before Thanksgiving break. It was already mid-October, and I knew there was no such thing as starting too early on prepping for a test at Canterwood. I'd have to find more time to add study time. I paged through my calendar, looking at everything I had going on this week.

Riding every day.

Glee club practice.

Meeting Cole outside of class to work on our assigned Lumière costume.

The list continued with smaller things like quizzes in different classes and a couple of essays due. I peered over my shoulder, and Khloe was bent over her math book, erasing furiously on her paper. *Take a breath,* I told myself. *If you stress, you'll get sick. Then nothing will get done. One thing at a time.*

The first thing that I needed was a cup of tea. I stood, putting my phone in my hoodie pocket, and slid my feet into gray fuzzy slippers.

"I'm going to make tea," I said. "Want anything from the common room?"

Khloe looked up, and she had that intense Khloe Kinsella *I'm studying so hard my brain might melt* look.

"I'll be your best friend until death do us part if you grab me a Diet Coke," Khloe said.

I smiled. "As long as it's until death do us part."

19

HALLWAY OF HORROR. KIND OF.

I OPENED THE DOOR, CLOSING IT QUIETLY behind me, and stared down the hallway. The Halloween decorations always made me feel better, no matter how stressed I was. Christina had to have spent *hours* and hours on the decorations. Stringy spider webbing draped just below the ceiling from one side of the hallway to the other. Black and purple plastic spiders sat in the webs.

Hairy bats that looked a little *too* real hung from random spots. Every bat had its wings in a different position. *Eeek!* I shivered and looked down. Fake or not, those bats looked ready to take off and zoom through the hallway.

Along the walls, foil cutouts of ghosts, witches, and pumpkins caught the light. Christina had taped cardboard pumpkins next to each door with our names written on them.

I stepped up to the hallway table along the wall, close to Christina's office. The decorated table was one of my favorite parts of the dorm. A giant glass jar of candy corn was next to a battery-operated grinning pumpkin. It smiled—missing a tooth—and next to it were beautiful gourds and real mini pumpkins. The entire table was covered in black, orange, and yellow confetti. A few ears of Indian corn were secured on the wall above the table.

Christina's office doorway was draped in teeny LED orange lights, which also decorated the common room. The lights, wrapped around the banister to the second floor, added a soft glow to the hallway.

I stepped into the empty common room. It was rare for no one else to be here, and I loved being alone in the comfy, spacious room. The couches and recliners had Halloween pillows—a friendly ghost, a black cat, a few pumpkins, and several square pillows with vampires or zombies stitched on them.

The windows had clings, just like the ones at the stable. I could stare at everything for hours! I opened the cabinet and got my teakettle. I filled it with water and turned on the stove. While I waited for the water to boil, I checked out the Halloween mug collection, trying to determine if there was one that I hadn't used yet.

Aha!

I reached behind a ghost mug and picked up a black mug with a set of vampire fangs painted on it.

Christina had also stocked the common room drawers with orange and black plasticware, plates, and napkins. Plastic Halloween cups filled one cabinet. Along the counter, jars held candy corn, a mismatch of candy like I got when I used to go trick-or-treating, caramel popcorn, cheese popcorn, and tiny round sugar cookies with orange frosting and black bat sprinkles.

I opened the jar of candy corn and reached inside. My phone vibrated in my jacket pocket.

I jumped, sucking in a fast breath. *Geeze, Lauren! You scared yourself with silly decorations, you nerd,* I thought as I fished out my phone. At least no one else had been witness to my silly scare.

It was a new BBM.

Drew:

Aw, it's sweet that u would feel bad 4 tagging me. But, if I remember correctly, I got you *3* times. Did u 4get abt that? ☺

I typed back right away.

Lauren:

*What?! 3x? Nooo. U got me 2x. Once when u had Cole help u corner me & then when u tagged me at the end. Did u srsly think I'd 4get being tagged? *smug smile**

Immediately, *Drew is typing a message* appeared on my phone.

Drew:

*Oh, LT. Srry, but ur smug smile is abt 2 be gooone. I got u when Clare cut u off, u tried 2 back up, & didn't know I was behind u. Ring any bells? *smug smile**

Oh, shoot! He was right. I'd completely forgotten about that tag. Ugggh. Now I had to fess up to remembering it.

Lauren:

hides face behind pillow* U r right. I *did* 4get abt that tag. That's what I get 4 sending a "la, la, la—I beat you!" BBM. *bows 2 u

I turned off the teakettle just as it started to whistle and left the kitchen. I'd get my tea in a minute. With a pumpkin pillow behind my back, I settled into the couch.

Drew:

LOL. I'll 4give u & 4get all abt the msg.

Lauren:

☺ *Thanks, D. That was only a TINY bit embarrassing.*

Drew:

I sent my BBM before I finished the next sentence! Meant 2 add I'll 4get abt it on ONE condition.

I grabbed one of the fleece Halloween-themed throws and pulled it over my legs.

Lauren:

What condition . . . ?

I couldn't imagine what Drew was going to ask me. It felt like forever before Drew's message appeared.

Drew:

Go out with me.

I grinned, wiggling my toes with excitement.

Lauren:

That's a horrible, mean condition. ;) Can't I do ur English hmwk 4 the wk? Or muck Polo's stall 4 a month?

Drew:

Lolol. U can do all of those—thank u for being so generous, Lauren. Date's a nonnegotiable, tho. Think u can put up with me 4 a few hours?

I loved this. Bantering with Drew was so easy and fun. He kept me on my toes. Drew always had a smart comeback when we teased each other, and he never took it too far. We both teased each other *just* enough and never in a mean way.

Lauren:

loud sigh I mean, I GUESS I could stomach hanging out w u. Anything in mind?

Drew:

☺ Cool. There r a ton of Halloween flicks playing on Fri night. U interested in seeing 1?

I dropped my teasing.

Lauren:

OMG, yes! I go to see a Halloween movie every year w my friends. Going w u sounds rlly fun.

Drew:

No way! I always go with my friends 2. But I'd rather go with you this year.

I smiled, my fingers hitting the wrong buttons as I tried to type fast while being so excited.

Lauren:

That's rlly sweet. ☺ I can't wait. What kind of movies r u into? Superscary? Psycho-thriller? Ones that try 2 b so scary that r actually silly?

Drew:

Bloody, crazy-scary Halloween movies rlly aren't my thing. That's lame, I know. I like the ones with teens who can't act—like We're Always Watching.

Lauren:

Hey, that's not lame, Drew. Srsly. I don't like violent movies

either. Not a fan of having 2 sleep w the lights on 4 nights aftr seeing a movie. I ♥ Watching. Seen it a bunch of times & it's my kind of movie, 2.

Drew:

U r a rlly cool girl, L. I've never told any1 but a couple of my friends abt my scary movie thing. I always make up an excuse if some1 asks me 2 see a rlly creepy movie.

Lauren:

I'd never make fun of u 4 not *liking* something. Srry u feel uncomfortable telling ppl who ask u 2 go.

Drew:

Well, *giant sigh,* I didn't want to see a supergross movie—Bones & Blood—at my old school. The guys started teasing me, and I ignored it. Whatever. Then they thought it was the best idea ever 2 try & scare me 4 days b4 Halloween. That's why I rlly don't tell any1.

I wished Drew was here. I wanted to hug him and make him a cup of tea.

Lauren:

That's awful! I'm so, so srry. Those ppl were losers w nothing better 2 do. U can watch—or not—any movie U want. Thanks 4 trusting me & telling me abt that. I won't tell any1.

Drew:

I know u won't. ☺

Lauren:

I'll share something w u that not many ppl know, if u want.

Drew:

Tell me.

Lauren:

Every year, my sister & I watch It's the Great Pumpkin, Charlie Brown. It's my #1 fave Halloween movie.

Drew:

R u kidding?

Oh, no. I shouldn't have told him that! Now he thought I was the biggest dork and—

Drew:

That's MY favorite movie! I've watched it on TV every yr since I could remember. ☺

Wheeew!

Lauren:

☺ *That's so neat that we both love that movie. Maybe we can watch it on TV or something, if you want.*

Drew:

For sure.

We chatted for a few more minutes before both having to sign off to tackle homework.

I made my tea, grabbed a soda for Khlo, and started to go back to my room. My phone vibrated again. I smiled, putting down the drinks. Drew must have had one more thing to say.

I opened BBM. It wasn't Drew. It was Ana.

Ana:

Hey, Laur. Can u talk tonite?

I glanced at the clock, biting my lip.

Lauren:

So sorry, A. I am BURIED under hmwk & can't. Tmrw?

Ana:

Okay. Call me 2mrw when u can. GL w ur hmwk.

Lauren:

Everything okay, tho? U okay?

Ana:

Totally!! Everything's fine—just wanted to chat. ☺ Love u!

Lauren:

Oh, good. Okay! Xxx

Soon I was absorbed in homework, fighting to keep myself from thinking about Friday. By the time I'd finished my homework, I could barely keep my eyes open as I washed my face the lazy way with an Olay face towelette and fell into bed.

20

PARFAIT SHIRT

I RAN MY FINGERS THROUGH MY NEWLY straightened hair, courtesy of one Khloe Kinsella.

"I love my hair, Khlo, thank you!" I said.

"No prob!" Khloe turned off the flatiron and left it out to cool off.

I turned on my lighted makeup mirror, so I could do a final makeup check. "Oh, KK, I pulled top options, and they're hanging inside my closet at the right end, starting on a purple hanger. Mind going through those and helping me pick?"

I looked into the mirror, adjusting it so I could see my roomie. She was nodding her head to the Top Forty pop songs that we had streaming from her laptop.

"I would only be the most honored roommate in

Hawthorne Hall to help you," Khloe said. "Let's see."

I stared at my reflection. Even though some girls in my classes used everything from foundation to eyeliner and heavy mascara, I was a fan of the natural look. I wanted to look as if I wasn't wearing much makeup—like I just happened to have zero zits or red spots.

Since it *was* date night, I'd added a few extra touches. A light dusting of shimmery gray eye shadow made my blue eyes look lighter. I'd dabbed off-white eye shadow from my Urban Decay palate into the corners of my eyes. It was one of my favorite EBTs: a little bit of white shadow made any eye look bigger. Also, it was my go-to when I'd been up too late the night before—it made me appear more awake in classes.

I'd curled my eyelashes, then applied one coat of black mascara. Eyes—check.

I used tinted moisturizer on my face. The ivory shade matched my skin tone and helped hide any blemishes. I squinted at the Enemy Pimple on my chin—I'd left it for last. It was a day old, and I'd been treating it with salicylic acid, which had reduced the size a little, but I still felt as if I had a red M&M on my chin.

I grabbed my green concealer—another EBT. Green canceled out red, Brielle had taught me, and I always used green concealer on pimples before blending in my usual concealer. I used my foundation brush to apply a small amount of green concealer. The green was *not* hiding the red! This wasn't the time for an EBT fail!

"KK," I moaned. "What if I can't hide this monster zit? I look like *I* belong in the horror movie that Drew and I are going to see! My green concealer EBT isn't working!"

"Laur, so not true—you don't look like a human who's contracted a flesh-eating disease and is wiping out the entire world population!"

"Khloe!"

Khloe hurried over, pulling her desk chair with her, and sat across from me. She looked at me, smiling. "Lauren, you're beautiful—that's what Drew's going to see. That zit is microscopic. But I know how you feel— it feels like it's huge and the only thing people see when they look at you."

I nodded. "Exactly."

"I'd never lie to you. It's not bad at *all*. Want me to do your concealer?"

"Please." I put down the brush, and Khloe got to work.

"This will take two seconds, and then I'll give you my final rec on a top," Khloe said. "Then we can decide what to pair with it—accessories, pants or skirt, shoes."

"You're the best."

"You know, I'll totally take that this time because . . . *voilà*! Check it!" Khloe grinned at me.

I looked in the mirror, closing one eye—afraid of what I'd see.

I saw . . . nothing.

I opened my other eye and looked closer. The pimple was *gone*.

"Khloe! *Oh, mon Dieu!*" I grabbed her in a hug, and she laughed.

"Not bad, huh? All of those hours doing stage makeup might have paid off just a tiny bit."

"Or a lot! You totally saved me from looking like I had a witch's wart on my chin."

Khloe shook her head and stood. "C'mon. Let's get you dressed, crazy girl."

All of the tops I'd narrowed down as options were spread on Khloe's bed.

"I'm stuck mainly between two," I said. "That purple boatneck with silver stitching and the gray tank top with sequins that I could throw a black cardigan over."

Khloe was quiet for a moment. "I don't think any of these work."

"What? Really? Um. Okay. I've got other tops." I

hurried over to my closet. "This one is pretty, right? The hunter green is a good color, and the capped sleeves are cute."

Khloe shook her head. "It's not right for this date."

I trusted Khloe's fashion advice a thousand percent. She was always honest, and it was why I trusted her so much—she'd never let me walk out the door looking silly.

"Officially panicking now. You choose some tops!"

"Think about this for a sec, Laur. What are you and Drew doing tonight?"

"Going to see a Halloween movie," I said slowly.

"Exactly. You have a fab collection of shirts that you only wear once a year. You didn't start wearing them until the middle of the month because you were afraid people would think you were a dork. But what happened instead?"

"You and the rest of my friends really like my Halloween shirts."

"*And* you've had other people tell you that they think your Halloween T-shirt collection is awesome. It's *you*. You're going on a date to see a Halloween movie. With a guy you really like. The only shirt that I'll give my SOA to is a Halloween shirt."

"Khloe," I said. "Are you *sure*? I'm going on a date. The shirts are perfect for classes and other stuff, but do you really think Drew will think I look okay in a Halloween shirt?"

She nodded. "More than okay. He'll love it because *you* love it. Move over."

Khloe stepped up to my closet, gently bumping her hip against mine. I sat on the edge of my bed, watching as she flipped through the section of my closet dedicated to Halloween tees. I was happy to see them out of their box and in my closet.

"I've got, as you would say, the *très parfait* shirt." Smiling, Khloe turned around, holding up her selection.

It was a white-neck tunic-length tee. A black cat sat tall on the bottom of the shirt, its emerald-colored eyes seeming to glow and its tail curled up along its body.

"Khloe, I don't even know what to say. I haven't worn that shirt yet, and it *is très parfait*! I didn't even consider one of those shirts."

"I know," Khloe said. "I'm really glad you're going to wear this. Halloween is *your* day—not just your favorite holiday, but your birthday, too. Drew will like anything you wear if you feel comfortable in it."

I stood, giving her a one-armed hug as I took the shirt. "You should be writing an advice column for *Girl!* magazine."

Khloe laughed. "Thanks, LT. Now I say either black leggings or black jeans."

"Jeans," I said. I pulled a pair from my dresser and laid them next to the shirt on my bed.

"I've got earrings in mind," Khloe said. "A necklace, too."

I changed into the top and jeans while Khloe went through her jewelry box. She held up a pair of silver drop earrings that were so fine, they were barely visible.

"Those are gorgeous," I said.

"I thought you could do simple earrings and a necklace like this one." Khloe walked over to me, and I looked at the necklace in her palm.

"You've got to be kidding!" I said. "No way!"

A quarter-size emerald stone cut into the shape of a heart with a delicate silver chain rested in her palm. The color of the stone matched the eyes of the cat on my shirt. *Exactly.*

Khloe grinned. "I saw it in this tiny boutique in Boston last summer when I was out with my friends. I didn't have enough allowance money, so I used my emergency credit card."

I grimaced. "You get in trouble?"

"Totally. No allowance for three months, but it was sooo worth it. Especially for moments like these!"

"Are you sure you don't mind if I borrow this?" I asked.

"I'll be offended if you don't."

"Thank you, thank you, Khlo."

I walked over to my full-length mirror and put on the earrings and necklace. The emerald had been cut so it caught light from every angle, and it seemed to glow around my neck.

"Wow," I said. "Khloe, the jewelry is . . . just so amazing." I turned so she could see.

An insta-smile came to her face. "You look great! I'm so excited!"

"Me too!" I glanced at the clock. "I need to hurry up or I'll be late."

"You're meeting at seven, right?" Khloe asked.

I nodded. "Inside the media center by the ticket counter."

Shoes were a no-brainer. I slid my feet into black ballet flats with tiny silver studs lining the crisscrossed leather over the closed toes.

I applied a quick coat of peachy gloss and a spritz of Vera Wang Princess perfume, then did one final mirror check. I felt comfy *and* pretty in my outfit. The combination of the two gave me a surge of confidence.

"You're set!" Khloe said. "You're going to have so

much fun! I'll be here when you get back, and you will be forced to tell me every detail. So don't forget a thing!"

Laughing, I grabbed my black shiny clutch that I'd already prepped for tonight and a light cardigan in case I got chilly.

"Trust me—I'll come back with every detail to share. Thank you again for everything."

"You're welcome, but go! If you keep thanking me, you really will be late."

With that, I left our room and hurried down Hawthorne's hallway. I'd already gotten permission from Christina to see a movie. She had extended my curfew to nine thirty as long as I stopped by her office to let her know that I was back.

I stepped outside, took a deep breath of the coolish air, and headed to the media center. I wasn't home to watch a movie with my friends or Becca, but I *did* have Drew. That made me smile as I passed a stack of hay bales with a scarecrow sitting on them. 'Tis the season!

21

IT'S NOT A TRICK
—IT'S A TREAT!

I STOOD JUST OUTSIDE THE MEDIA CENTER, watching students enter and exit—the smell of buttery popcorn drifting outside each time the door opened. After one more deep breath, I made myself go inside.

Drew, already waiting, smiled as I walked over to him. He looked incredibly cute in a burnt orange polo shirt and jeans.

"Hey," he said. "I love your shirt."

I said a silent thank you to Khloe and one aloud to Drew.

"Let's get drinks and snacks," Drew said.

At the counter, we got a large tub of popcorn to share, Diet Cokes, Peanut M&Ms, and Twizzlers.

"Let me grab the tickets," Drew said, starting toward the counter.

"No, let me," I said.

Drew shook his head. "This one's on me. You can get the next one. Deal?"

I finally conceded. "Deal."

It didn't take long for Drew to grab two tickets, and we walked to the last screening room. Inside, every red seat was empty.

"That's so weird," I said. "Are we ridiculously early? Or did we miss a memo that the movie wasn't showing or something?"

"I think we're right on time," Drew said, smiling. "Don't worry."

He let me pick our seats and I put my drink in the holder, the popcorn between us, and opened my Twizzlers. Still, not one student came through the doors. The rope lighting lining the aisles started to dim along with the overhead lights.

"I think we're in the wrong place," I said. "We're the only ones here!"

Drew turned, smiling, and took my hand. "That's kind of how I planned it."

I shook my head, confused. Drew's hand on mine wasn't exactly helping, either! "What are you talking about?"

"Just wait," Drew said.

The theater went completely dark, and the movie started. At the first note of the familiar music, I squeezed Drew's hand, gaping at the screen. *It's the Great Pumpkin, Charlie Brown* was playing.

"Oh my God. Drew. I can't believe you did this. How?"

"I remembered what you told me about this movie. We *could* have watched it on TV, but I talked to the manager, and he said he'd play this film for us."

I shook my head in disbelief. This was beyond amazing. Drew *really* listened to me. I wondered if a better Halloween could exist.

"This is the sweetest thing anyone's ever done for me," I said. "I really don't know what to say."

Drew's entire face had an unmistakable happy glow. "You don't have to say anything. Just watch with me."

I snuggled back into my chair, holding Drew's hand as we watched Lucy draw a pumpkin face on the back of Charlie's head. I lost myself in the cartoon, but at the same time, didn't forget for a second who was sitting beside me. This was definitely the best treat I ever had.

22

HE'S MY BOY FRIEND.
NOT *BOYFRIEND*.

Lauren Towers's Blog

6:44 p.m.: Where are you, tomorrow?

I think time has STOPPED. Okay, okay. I know that sounds ridiculous and I'm not insane, but I *do* think there's a possibility that time is moving slower. I don't think tomorrow's ever going to get here! This entire week has crept by ever since my date last weekend.

(I just reread that paragraph, and I think some of K's drama-queen attitude rubbed off on me! JK, K! You know I ♥ you! ☺)

At least tomorrow, I'll have more to keep me busy. Like party prep! K already told me that she, L, C, J, and a bunch of our other friends will be "gone" for a while. "Gone" is code for "We're setting up for your birthday party!" K's out now, "helping Lex with math homework." LOL. K pulled off the lie in the acting department, but not in the excuse area. Homework on a Friday night? Um, never! At least I had homework earlier in the week to keep me busy.

But I am the luckiest girl ever. I've got a roomie who's my bestie, and she's excited about my birthday like it's her own. Plus, my other friends have been helping. It means so much that they're helping to put together a party for *me*. And I know my friends are doing it in their free time, which isn't much at CC. I know tomorrow night's going to be the best birthday/Halloween ever. E-V-E-R. Can't think of a better combo. ☺

There *is* a part of it, though, that's bittersweet. A, B, and Sister B won't be there. Neither will Mom or Dad. Not that they were at my last few b-day parties, but I've always *seen* them on my birthday. This year, I'll just hear their voices. It makes me homesick to think about it. That's the last thing A, B, Sister B, and my parents would want me to feel tomorrow. They'll all want me to have fun with my new friends and enjoy my favorite holiday.

I wonder what it will feel like to turn thirteen. I absolutely cannot wait for someone to ask, "How old are you?" and I'll say, "Thirteen." Very nonchalant. It *looks* cool even on the computer! ☺ I'm going to be THIRTEEN tomorrow! K said a bigger, more important birthday doesn't exist. Except for sixteen. But I can barely process thirteen—sixteen can wait a while!

Going to log off and beg K for a detail about tomorrow. Just one! A tiny one! Wish me luck.

Posted by Lauren Towers

I closed my laptop and settled onto my bed. I grabbed the latest issue of *Flirt!* and flipped through the pages. Usually I read the mag from cover to cover—not skipping one section. I always learned something new from the latest It Products in makeup or a new hot oil hair treatment voted Best New Find by the magazine editors.

My phone chimed. *Yes!* Hopefully, it was one of my friends who wanted to BBM or Skype.

It was Taylor.

Taylor:

Hey, L! Wanted 2 say hi & c what ur doing 4 ur bday 2mrw.

I typed back.

Lauren:

Hi, Tay. ☺ *My friends are throwing me a party. Kind of a big deal—it's a masquerade party.*

Taylor:

179

Whoa. That's cool! Knowing u—u must have found an awesome mask and dress.

I'd told Bri and Ana a few days ago over BBM, but they clearly hadn't mentioned it to Taylor.

Lauren:

Thx. ☺ I got really lucky—found my dream dress in a mag and got it online. Then I looked for a mask to match and found a really, really pretty pink one with pearls and feathers.

Taylor:

I bet you'll look great. A masquerade party sounds like the perfect way to celebrate. I'm glad ur friends r doing this 4 u.

Lauren:

They're the best. I'm sooo excited! Kind of sad, too, at the same time. First bday w/o Becs and Mom and Dad. Missing Bri, Ana and

I stopped midsentence. I was going to write "you, too." But it didn't feel right. I missed Taylor—like a friend. Not an ex-boyfriend that I wanted back. Plus, I really, really like-liked Drew, and it felt weird to tell Tay that I missed him. I went back to the message, retyping the last part.

Lauren:

They're the best. I'm sooo excited! Kind of sad, too, at the same time. First bday w/o Becs and Mom and Dad. Missing Bri & Ana. And it'll b weird that u and my other Union friends won't b there.

Taylor:

I understand the mixed feelings. I know B and A will be thinking abt u. I'm happy 4 u and I know ur gonna have a great party.

Lauren:

☺ I think it'll be fun. What r u doing this wkend?

Taylor:

Superbusy, actually. Going w Dad on a road trip.

Lauren:

Ugh. Is he dragging u along 2 a biz thing?

Taylor:

I volunteered 2 go. Actually, made him rlly happy. So after tmrw, I hope he'll ease up on me abt becoming Mr. Frost, VP of Dad's Company.

Lauren:

Good thinking. I'll cross my fingers 4 u.

Taylor:

Gotta run, but TTYS. I have a feeling ur going 2 have a RLLY awesome bday. ☺

Lauren:

Thanks! Talk soon! ☺

I exited BBM, leaning back against my pillow and hoping Taylor was right. The doorknob turned and Khloe stepped inside. She smiled at me.

"Hey," she said. "What have you been up to?"

"Blogging and BBMing Taylor," I said. "How was math with Lexa?"

Khloe kicked off her ballet flats and flopped onto her bed. "Oh, hard. You know. Math."

I bit back a grin. "Did you use her book? I saw yours was on your desk."

Khloe tucked a blond piece of hair behind her ear. "I didn't want to carry mine, so I used Lex's."

"Yeah, carrying it down the hallway is tough," I said, struggling to keep a straight face.

Khloe nodded. In the light, specks of silver glitter sparkled on her cheek.

I sat up, peering at her face. "Is that a new makeup trend that I missed?"

Khloe froze. "What . . . do you mean? Exactly."

"The sparkles! They look so pretty on your cheek!"

Her hands flew to her face and she swiped both cheeks, then looked at her hands.

"It's something that kind of happened accidentally," she said. "Lex had a project due for art, and I touched it before the glue was dry. Totally didn't realize I got it on my face." Khloe laughed. "Oops!"

I decided to stop playing with her. She *was* working on my party, after all.

Khloe got cleaned up and into pj's. A bright orange oversize tee and black leggings.

She rolled on her side and looked at me.

"Taylor's been BBMing you a lot lately," Khloe said. "And he called that one day."

"We're still friends," I said. "Brielle and Ana have been kind of MIA recently, so it's been nice to hear from someone at home."

"I hope this doesn't make you sad or anything, but do you know if he's dating anyone?" Khloe asked.

"He hasn't said anything to me. If he was with someone, Bri or Ana would totally tell me."

"Does Taylor know about Drew?" Khloe asked.

"We don't really talk about that stuff. I guess I didn't want to make Tay feel bad if he wasn't dating anyone and I told him I was going out with Drew. Not that we're official or anything."

Khloe got up, grabbing a Diet Dr Pepper from our mini-fridge.

"Do you think you still have feelings for Taylor?" she asked.

"What? No. No way. You know the breakup was mutual, and I feel lucky that Tay's still willing to be my friend. He's *just* a friend, though."

"Just asking," Khloe said. "I didn't think you had feelings for him since you're into Drew, but it can happen.

I'm glad for you that you've got a friend from home who's there if Brielle or Ana are busy or something."

"Me too."

Khloe started telling me about this rumor that she'd heard from Clare about this guy in our English class, but I zoned out. Khloe's questions about Taylor kept going through my head. *I* didn't still like-like him. He was my friend. But what if he felt something different? What if Taylor still wanted me to be his girlfriend?

". . . and isn't that insane?" Khloe asked.

"Mm-hmm," I said. "Crazy."

Khloe picked right back up with her story. I knew what I needed to do: The next time Taylor BBMed or called, I had to tell him that I'd been going out with Drew. That was something that I'd tell a friend, and that's exactly what Taylor was to me.

23

OFFICIALLY THIRTEEN!

"HAPPY BIRTHDAY!" I JUMPED, OPENING MY eyes and seeing a grinning Khloe standing beside my bed.

I smiled and *that* feeling washed over me. The it's-my-birthday feeling.

"Thank you! Ahh! I'm sooo excited!"

"You've got to get up and come with me to the common room," Khloe said. "The celebration of LT begins right now!"

"Eeee!" I squealed. "Yay!"

I pulled on sky-blue lounge pants and a T-shirt with a cupcake with pink frosting and a candle. I ran a brush through my hair and pulled it into a ponytail.

Khloe waited by the door. She looked as if she'd been up for hours, and it was only ten.

I slipped on flip-flops and followed her to the common room.

The door was shut. I glanced at Khloe.

"The door's never closed," I said. Excitement bubbled in my stomach.

"Then you better open it."

I turned the knob, slowly opening the door and stepping inside.

"HAPPY BIRTHDAY, LAUREN!"

Confetti rained down on me as my friends cheered and clapped.

My mouth felt stuck open, and I still held the doorknob, not moving.

"Get in here, LT!" Clare said, waving me over. "You have to *be* in here to join the breakfast party."

"You guys!" I said.

Khloe laughed, gently pushing me forward. The shock wore off, and I looked at everyone who had shown up this morning for *me*.

Clare.

Lexa.

Jill.

And Khloe, of course.

The room was full of black, purple, and orange

bunches of balloons. A HAPPY BIRTHDAY sign hung above the fireplace.

"I can't believe you did this," I said to everyone. "The party tonight is more than enough. You didn't have to throw me a breakfast party too!"

Everyone giggled. They were all dressed in cheery lounge clothes—lots of bright colors that made me happy to look at.

"Please," Jill said. "If you call this a 'party,' that would be really insulting. Balloons and a banner are so not enough." Lexa's roomie smiled at me.

"Ooh, forgot one thing," Clare said. She hurried into the kitchen and turned on my teakettle.

They were even making me tea!

"What Jill said," Lex added, grinning. "You obviously have nooo idea how Canterwood girls party."

"But you will tonight!" Clare said. Her long hair was in a cute side braid secured by a glittery purple elastic.

"Come sit!" Khloe said, taking my hand and pulling me forward and onto the couch.

The table in front of us was full of breakfast food. There was a bowl of mixed fruit and giant lidded plates with steam coming through the hole in the top of the metal lids. A basket of various croissants, muffins, and doughnuts was filled to the brim. Five empty tea mugs were clustered together.

"Thanks to Christina," Jill said, "we have eggs, pancakes, waffles, sausage, and bacon under the lids."

"Omigosh," I said. "It's a feast!"

Then I saw plates, napkins, and plastic silverware. It made my eyes watery. It was all sky blue.

"You are the best friends ever," I said. "Every detail about this is perfect. You got all of this in my favorite color. I'm still new here, and the way you're treating my birthday makes me feel so special."

"We love our LT," Khloe said, squeezing my arm. "It doesn't matter to me, and probably everyone else in this room, how long you've been here. Speaking for myself, I've gotten to know you really well, and it feels like we've been friends forever, not just since September."

I smiled. "I feel the same way about all of you."

The teakettle whistled, and Khloe got up and turned it off. She carried over my tea basket and lowered it in front of me.

"Birthday girl chooses the tea," Khlo said.

"You guys really thought of everything," I said. I looked at my tea selection, knowing exactly what I wanted.

I picked up a box of pumpkin spice tea. "My mom

makes a cup of this for me every year on my birthday," I said. "It's so good—it reminds me of fall, and I don't have it all year until my birthday."

"Pumpkin spice it is," Lexa said. "That sounds really good."

I started to open the box of tea, but Lexa swatted at my hand.

"Um, nooo. You start filling your plate for breakfast," Lexa said. "We've got the tea covered."

"Thanks," I said. I handed over the box.

The girls got up, taking all of the mugs with them, and started filling mugs with water, adding tea bags, and pouring a packet of Splenda into each cup.

Khloe set mine in front of me, and I smiled my appreciation. We all loaded our pretty plates with a variety of breakfast foods.

"So, we have something planned with breakfast," Khloe said. I took a bite of a strawberry, looking at her. "Becca and I have been in touch."

"I knew it!" I said, laughing. "There's no way my sister would *not* contact you about today."

"She was really bummed that she couldn't be here to celebrate your birthday," Khloe continued. "Your parents and Ana and Brielle were too."

Khloe's words made my chest tighten. I'd never had a birthday without my family. Even though today couldn't have started off more wonderful, I still missed them.

Khloe reached beside her and held up a purple plastic DVD case. It was covered in stickers—unicorns, hearts, smiley faces, and cupcakes. Khloe handed it to me and through the plastic, I saw a folded piece of paper with LAUREN written on it.

"You're supposed to read the note, and then we'll watch the DVD," Khloe said.

Everyone watched as I opened the case and unfolded the note. Immediately, I recognized Becca's handwriting.

"Can I read it aloud?" I asked.

Each girl nodded.

"'Little Sister,'" I started. "'Happy, happy birthday! I can't believe you're turning thirteen. OMG, I'm going to have a teenage sister to deal with when you come home this summer. There's lots I want to say, but it won't fit on this note. Mom and Dad were going to send you a card, but um, they didn't want to write you "Happy Birthday." Instead, they—oh, forget it. Just pop in the DVD, 'kay? Love always, Becs.'"

"Aw!" everyone chorused.

I blinked to clear my vision, which had been blurred by

tears. "Becs is the best. That was so sweet." I reread the note. "I'm kind of confused about my parents, though," I said.

Khloe held out a hand. "I think the DVD might clear that up."

She put the DVD in the player and sat beside me. The screen on the giant plasma was black, then a bright purple filled the screen, with HAPPY BIRTHDAY, LAUREN! in aqua font. I left my breakfast on my lap, untouched. I didn't want to miss a second.

"Happy birthday to you!" Mom, Dad, and Becca came onto the screen. I couldn't stop the tears as they sang the entire "Happy Birthday" song. Wordlessly, Clare put a tissue in my hands. It felt as though I was home and in the living room with them. They were seated together on the couch. I took in every little detail almost as if I'd never seen my home before. Every candle, every pillow, every photo was in the exact same place as it had been when I'd left. That made me feel good.

"And now," Becca said, "Mom and Dad have a few things to say."

Becca got up and moved off camera. I noticed the navy lace dress with a wide belt—it was new. *That* made me excited. Becca would have a ton of new clothes, and I'd "accidentally" pack a few of them in my suitcase on the way back to school.

"Hi, honey," Mom said.

"LaurBell!" Dad chimed in. "Hi, sweetheart."

I'd heard my parents' voices so many times since I'd been at Canterwood, and I'd even seen them through Skype, but nothing compared to this. Skype had its moments of breaking up, and the clarity wasn't the best. The video was amazingly sharp.

Mom was in a pretty, sandy-colored blouse, and Dad was in the T-shirt that I'd bought him for Christmas one year. A gray tee with black letters that said BE CAREFUL OR YOU MIGHT END UP IN MY NOVEL!

"Lauren, your dad and I wish we could celebrate your birthday with you. Turning thirteen is a milestone in life. You will always be our little girl in our hearts. In reality, you have grown into a strong, smart, loving, and beautiful daughter. I could not be more proud of you for all you've accomplished at such a young age."

I sniffled. Mom and I had a complicated relationship. Sometimes I felt she paid more attention to work than me. But everything she'd said made me realize that my mom loved me more than I thought.

Mom sniffed and dabbed her eyes with a tissue. "If

your dad and I *had* to miss your birthday, the best excuse in the world is having you be away at Canterwood Crest Academy. I think about you every day, Lauren, and miss you. But I am prouder than I could ever express that you are following your dreams. I love you, sweetie, and can't wait to see you soon at Family Weekend. Oh, and I've heard from Becca that your new friends have planned quite the party for you—so I want to thank them and can't wait to hear all about it."

Mom looked at Dad, and he was teary like Mom! I was used to that from Dad—he was the softie between the two of them. I quickly glanced at the girls—they were all teary. Clare was dabbing her pink nose with a tissue.

"Lauren, LaurBell, Laurbaby," Dad said. His gentle voice made me feel as if he was hugging me. "You're thirteen today. Thirteen. Time couldn't have gone by any faster. Today I'm thinking about all of the time you and I spent on the road together, traveling for your shows, and how grateful I am that we had those moments together. You'd be asleep in one bed, alarm clock set for five in the morning, having fallen asleep with a book on your chest. I'd be in the next bed or at the desk writing my latest book and thinking how lucky I was to have a job where I could travel with my daughter."

Dad took a breath, looking down and then back at the camera. I watched him, my chin trembling. "I wouldn't have changed one thing about the journey you took from your first pony ride until now," he continued. "I hope you have zero regrets and are proud of the person you've become. For this birthday, I wish that you'd know even a little bit how much I love you."

"Okay, Dad!" Becca's voice rang through our living room. She stepped in front of the camera, giving me an *I'm so sorry about our parents!* look.

Becca perched on the armchair. "This is where I'm supposed to give the big-sister speech. You know, I love you. Proud of you, etc. Before I talk, I think I'll let *our* big sister say a few words."

"What?" I said aloud, unable to keep the thought to myself.

The screen went dark for a split second, then Charlotte's face appeared onscreen. She was in her dorm—I recognized posters of her favorite singers and plays. The walls were a light pastel purple, and a wire rack that said DREAM hung on the wall, holding some of her purses.

I couldn't believe she'd done this for me. She wasn't even in Union—Char was away at Sarah Lawrence College.

"Heeeey, Laur!" Charlotte's tan, pretty face smiled.

"Happy number thirteen! I can't believe this day is here—really." She grimaced. "I mean, all of those times I dropped you as a baby . . ." She laughed. "Just kidding! So, what do you think of my hair?" Charlotte spun around in her desk chair. Her California blond hair had been down almost to the middle of her back the last time I saw her. Now it was a chin-length bob.

"Cute, right?" Char said, fluffing it with a wink. "I chopped it off last week and donated it to Locks of Love. Anyway, I can't really call you my baby sister anymore. I remember the day I turned thirteen—it was a Friday, and my friend, Lysa, threw me a sleepover at her house. I was the first one in my group of friends to turn thirteen, and I felt *so* cool." Charlotte laughed. "Poor Mom and Dad. I spent about a month being 'wild,' then I got bored and turned back into the Charlotte you know and love."

I smiled. This was the biggest surprise on the DVD. Charlotte and I had a rocky relationship. It was getting better, but I knew that part of her still resented me for traveling so much. Dad usually went with me because of my age, and Char didn't see much of him when it was show season. Maybe this DVD was the start of taking steps to repair our relationship.

"Have an awesome party, a wonderful birthday, and I'll chat with you tomorrow. Love you, Laur."

The screen flickered to black, and Becca appeared. She was sitting on her bed, the camera probably perched on a stack of books.

"Surprised?" Becs asked. She grinned. "I thought so. I wanted to be the one to tell you that per your super-selfless request, we've all donated to the horse charity that Khloe sent us in an e-mail. Unlike the rest of the fam, who took, like, three hours of your day, I'm keeping my message short. You know I love you. You're the best sister in the world, and no matter where you're spending your birthday, I'm thinking about you. I kind of feel like I'm already there, since Khloe and I have been e-mailing so much and she walked me through every detail of the party."

I grinned at Khloe. "You two," I said.

"I'll see you *very* soon during Family Weekend, and I can't wait to give you a belated birthday hug. Now go have fun!"

The screen faded to black, and I was still for a moment, taking in everything that had just happened. I *knew* Becs had been the one to organize and make the DVD. It was a present I could keep always and watch whenever I got homesick for my family.

I looked around, realizing none of us had touched our breakfast. These girls really cared—they'd watched every minute of the DVD along with me.

"That was the best gift from my family. Ever," I said.

"Well, that's not *exactly* it," Clare said.

She reached behind the couch pillow and pulled three envelopes—pink, purple, and blue—from the hiding spot.

We leaned toward each other, and I took the cards from her. I recognized my mom and dad's, Becs's, and Charlotte's handwriting. "I think I'll save these for later," I said. "I've exposed you to enough of the Towers family, for the morning at least."

The girls nodded. "Jill, you want to grab that thing from the pantry?" Khloe asked.

Jill jumped up so fast, she almost knocked the plate of food off her lap.

"You guys . . . ," I said. "It better not be a present."

The girls looked at each other. "We promise," Lexa started. "We all donated to the thoroughbred charity. This is a tiny something from all of us."

Jill set a cellophane-wrapped basket in front of me. "Think of it as something for all of us. We can share!"

I untied the ribbon from the basket and pulled away the plastic. Inside a wooden woven basket was an assortment of teas. Green. Black. White. Red. Oolong. Chai. Herbal.

"This was something you knew I couldn't turn down," I said. "You used my weakness against me!"

We laughed, and I smiled at them. "Thank you, really. I can't wait to try all of these."

We finished breakfast, and the girls refused to let me help clean up. When they'd finished, I stood and joined them near the door.

"I think it's time to chill, shower—whatever," Khloe said. "Just make sure you're at the ballroom by seven or I'll hunt you down."

We separated in the hallway, and Khloe shut our door behind me, bouncing on her toes. "Are you ready for party prepping?"

"So ready!" I put my DVD present on my desk.

"I mean, *really* ready. You'll be showering, shampooing, doing your nails, and a million other things to get ready for your *thirteenth* birthday."

"Khlo! You're making me nervous!" I fell onto my back on my bed.

"Lauren Towers! Do not lie down!" Khloe had a drill-sergeant-like voice. "You will get up, get in the shower, and Operation Birthday and Halloween Party will commence."

I smiled, letting her pull me off the bed and onto my feet.

I stepped into the bathroom, started to close the door, then stuck out my head. "I have this feeling that tonight's going to be amazing."

Khloe smiled. "I hope it's everything you wished for."

24

ANA SPILLS

I laughed, watching my friend frown as we Skyped. Khloe and I were taking a break from prepping for tonight. I'd gotten a bunch of texts from Ana and Brielle and wanted to talk to them before tonight. I'd tried Brielle via BBM, text, and even calling her at home, but she was MIA. I'd called Ana next. I realized, too, that I'd never called her when she asked me to days ago. Things were so busy, and I was focused on Halloween and my birthday.

"What's weird?" I asked.

"You're a *teen*. That sounds so cool. You can walk around and think 'I'm a teen. Yep. I'm not a kid or a tween. I'm a T-E-E-N.' I'm still stuck with the 'tween' label for a few months." Ana batted her eyelashes. "Are you still going to be friends with me?"

"Hmm." I tapped my forehead, pretending to think. "I guess I'll be friends with a *tween*. You're lucky that you're turning thirteen soon, though. Otherwise, I'd have to reconsider."

Ana shook her head. "Have you talked to Bri?"

"She left me a happy birthday message and I've been trying to get in touch, but I can't. Do you know where she is?"

I thought an odd or maybe guilty look flashed on Ana's face. But she smiled and leaned closer to the webcam.

"I'm totally not supposed to tell you this," she said. "But Bri's at the hair salon."

"And you're not supposed to say anything because . . . ?"

Ana reached beside her computer, grabbed a lip gloss, and smoothed some Rosebud Salve on her lips.

"Annnaaa," I said. "You have to tell me now. If Bri's getting a trim, it's really not a big secret!"

Again, I swore a look came over Ana's face, but it disappeared before I could be sure.

"It's not a trim," she said. "It's *huge*. I know she wanted to tell you herself, but you can't get ahold of her, so I'm telling you." Ana grinned. "Brielle's going BLOND!"

"What? Did you just say 'blond'?"

Ana nodded. "Like, *blond* blond. She booked the appointment a couple of weeks ago, and it's going to take, like, four hours."

"Oh my God! I can't even imagine *Brielle* as a blonde! Her hair is *raven black*! It's going to take so much bleach and color. When did she decide to do it? How'd she get her parents to say yes? What do you think?"

"Bri said she was superbored and wanted a change. I think it was a couple of weeks ago because that's when she got an appointment."

"I can't believe she didn't say anything to me about it," I said. "Honestly, my feelings are a little hurt. I'd talk to you guys before I did something drastic."

Ana nodded. "I'm sorry, Laur. I'd feel the same way. I know Bri wasn't purposely *not* telling you. I think she was caught up in making the decision, convincing her parents, and then showing you, maybe like a big reveal."

I took a breath. "I'm not there every day, either. Bri and I haven't talked much lately and she might feel that whole 'out of sight, out of mind' thing."

Ana was silent. She looked down and opened and closed her mouth several times.

"Ana, I'm sorry. What I said to you wasn't fair. Brielle

is your best friend, and it wasn't cool for me to complain about our issues to you. I really am sorry to have put you on the spot."

Ana rested her chin on her hand. "It's okay. This whole thing is hard. We're all learning how to deal with you being gone. It's kind of like a long-distance relationship!"

"It's definitely like that. But I think we're doing a pretty good job, and I am so happy to 'see' you on my birthday."

That made Ana grin. "Agreed. Okay, so, let me tell you the rest. Bri studied all of these magazines, figured out the color that she wanted, how much it was going to cost, why she should be allowed to have it done, and then she, wait for it, made a *PowerPoint* presentation!"

"Brielle? Omigod. Keep going!"

"She did! She practiced it with me a few times and then showed her parents. They were impressed with all of the thought Bri had put into it. Her mom told her to give them a couple of days to discuss it and they would let her know."

"I can't believe they said yes. It has to be pretty expensive, and Bri's going to need touch-ups and stuff like that."

Brielle was lucky, like Ana and me, that her family

wasn't hurting for money. But our parents never handed us anything either. That was one of the things that had bonded us at Yates Prep—a school filled with students of privilege.

"I think that's why Bri's parents ultimately said yes," Ana said. "Bri promised a bunch of things, like As in all of her classes, doing more chores around the house, *and* working at the salon every Saturday to help pay for some of the cost."

"The salon gave her a job? Seriously? Do they know she's twelve?"

"Get this," Ana said. "Brielle had a 'meeting' with the owner and the manager of the salon, and the owner, Suzi, agreed. Bri can only work for three hours every weekend, and she'll just be sweeping up hair, mopping—stuff like that."

"Wait. If she's spending three hours at the salon on Saturday, when is she riding?"

"Oh, she's been riding at a different time than me for a while now. I totally forgot to tell you. She's riding in the evening, and she started taking private lessons on Sunday morning."

"Oh." I tried not to sound or look as hurt as I felt. "That's cool. I'm glad Bri's not missing riding *and* that she's getting to go blond."

Ana and I spent a few more minutes exchanging semi-uncomfortable small talk.

"I've better get off Skype," I said. "I have to get ready for tonight."

Ana smiled. "You're going to have so much fun. I can't wait to hear every detail!"

"I'm really excited. I'm sure somebody will post pics on FaceSpace, too."

"I'll be looking. And hey, I'm *so* sorry that my present and card didn't get there today. Bri and I sent ours together, and we mailed them a day too late."

"It's okay. It'll give me something else to look forward to!"

We said good-bye and hung up. I realized too late that Ana hadn't brought up whatever she'd wanted me to call her about. *Maybe I should call her back,* I thought. *If it was that important, though, Ana would have tried to talk to me again way before now.*

I let all of it go, including the Blond Brielle ordeal, and let my thoughts drift to my party.

25

BEST. EBTS. EVER.

LATER ON, KHLOE AND I WERE IN OUR ROBES, our dresses hanging on our closet doors. We'd both showered and dried our hair. Styling would come later.

All day I'd been fielding texts from Canterwood friends, Brielle, Ana, Becs, Char, and my parents. I promised Bri and Ana that I'd call them and had texted thank-yous to Becca, Charlotte, and my parents for the DVD.

While Khloe was in the shower, I'd used the alone time to open my cards. My parents and sisters had given me a gift card to Macy's, and I was already itching to get online to look at clothes.

Everyone had written sweet messages that had made me cry. I'd felt like a huge baby, but I missed home. I tried to remind myself that I did have Whisper and she was a part of Union and Briar Creek. Thinking about Wisp had cheered me up, and by the time she'd gotten out of the shower, Khloe hadn't noticed that I'd been upset.

Khloe's phone beeped and she swiped it, glancing at the screen. "Okay, I have to tell you something," she said. She gave me a larger-than-usual smile.

Uh-oh.

"Khloeee," I said, standing and crossing my arms. "What did you do?"

Khloe hopped from foot to foot. "I know you said no presents, but—"

"Khloe!" I shook my head. "I was serious. I don't need anything. You, Lex, Clare, and Jill already donated to the retired racehorse charity—it's *all* that I want."

There was a knock on our door. I stared at Khloe with wide eyes.

"I can't exactly take it back," Khloe said. "And I think it's something you're *really* going to like."

She hurried to the door, and I expected to see Christina or a delivery person when she opened the door. Instead, a smiling woman with fiery red streaks in her black hair smiled at us.

"Khloe?" she asked.

"Yes," Khloe said. "Whitney, right?"

The woman—Whitney—nodded. I saw a bag over her shoulder and two giant black cases with silver latches.

"Hi," Whitney said to me. "I bet you're the birthday girl, Lauren."

I nodded, still not sure what was going on. "Nice to meet you."

"C'mon in," Khloe said. "Put your stuff anywhere."

Whitney was dressed in a black V-neck sweater with sequin lining and skinny jeans. She set her bag on the ground and the cases beside it.

"Who's going first?" Whitney asked, looking between Khloe and me.

"Um," I finally said. "I'm sorry. I don't know what's going on."

"Ooops!" Khloe said, giggling. "Lauren, Whitney is a professional makeup artist. Since this is your big night, I didn't want you to worry about doing your makeup. It's kind of a present for both of us, since Whitney's doing my makeup and yours."

"Wait. What? You got us a *makeup* artist?" I *had* to have misheard her.

Khloe gave me a tiny nod.

"Omigod!" I threw my arms around Khloe. "I said no

presents, but *this* is beyond awesome. We're going to look amazing and perfect for the party."

Khloe grinned. "I'm so glad you're not mad at me."

"How could I be? Having my makeup done by a professional makes me feel like a celebrity. Like we're about to go to the most glam party ever!"

Khloe pointed me toward my desk chair. "*You* are a celeb tonight. And hey, you haven't seen the party planning skills of Canterwood girls. We throw the most glam parties on the East Coast."

I sat down in my chair, and Whitney stood. She'd been crouched on the floor, opening her black cases, which had revealed the most makeup I'd ever seen. Khloe pulled out our nail polish collection and spread out everything at the end of her bed.

"Your skin is gorgeous, Lauren," Whitney said. "Mind putting your hair in a ponytail for me?"

"Thank you, and no problem." I pulled back my hair, and Whitney opened a pack of foundation sponges.

"Your skin is even enough that I'm going to use a mousse type of foundation that's incredibly light and sheer," Whitney said. "If there's anything you don't like, tell me and we'll not only fix it, but I'll make it even better."

"That sounds good," I said.

"What's the color of your dress?" Whitney asked. "I want to make sure I don't choose any makeup shades that will clash."

I pointed to my dress, on a padded hanger hooked over my closet door.

"That's beautiful!" Whitney said. "Mind if I take a look?"

"Not at all!"

Whitney looked at my dress, touching the fabric and looking at the sequins.

"Did you choose this yourself?" she asked.

"I found it online," I said. "I'd looked at what felt like a million dresses, and none of them felt right. Then I saw this one, and I fell in love with it from the cut to the color."

"Are you interested in fashion?" Whitney asked, stepping back to her makeup kits. "I hope so!"

I smiled. "I *love* fashion. I'm taking an intro course this year. I'm learning to sew and am making a costume with a partner for the school's fall play."

Whitney, Khloe, and I fell into a long conversation while Whitney started my makeup. Khloe didn't know that she'd hired a makeup artist who also did makeup for several up-and-coming stars, including a Broadway actor that Khloe was *obsessed* with.

"Pause," Khloe said, holding up a freshly manicured hand. "Those brushes have touched Nadia Reese's face? Oh. My. God."

Whitney laughed. "They have been cleaned since then, but yes."

The look in Khloe's eyes was far away, as if she hadn't heard Whitney. "Those brushes touched Nadia Reese," Khloe repeated in a whisper.

Whitney and I traded smiles as she did my makeup, and Khloe stayed in a dreamlike state. The process was calming, almost like a massage. Whitney used at least half a dozen different-size brushes to apply everything from concealer to eye shadow.

"See what you think!" Whitney said, handing me a mirror.

"Ooh, Lauren!" Khloe said, clasping her hands. She watched as I held the mirror in front of me. I stared, wide-eyed, at my reflection.

"Whoa." I blinked and peered closer at myself. "It's *exactly* what I wanted, Whitney! Thank you! Thank you!"

Whitney's bright red lips parted into a giant smile. "Oh, I'm so glad. It's your thirteenth birthday party, and

I wanted your makeup to *enhance* your beauty, not cover you up."

Khloe hopped off her bed and put her face inches from mine. "Wow, *wow*. Laur, you look just like you except ready to party!"

True to her word, Whitney had kept my foundation light. My skin didn't look buried under a layer of caked-on makeup. Any blemishes were gone, and my skin tone was even.

My eyelids had been dusted in a light gray with a silver shimmer. A coat of mascara and curled lashes made my eyes look wider.

I made a mental note to ask Whitney for any EBTs she could share—especially about eyes. Khloe and I *did* have an expert in our room—we'd be crazy not to ask for tips!

Peachy blush had been dusted on the apples of my cheeks and my cheekbones. An almost-matching gloss felt smooth on my lips and added a hint of color.

"I want you to keep this," Whitney said, picking up a tube of gloss. "It's the shade you're wearing, and now you'll be able to reapply it as needed tonight."

Thanking her, I took the gloss and hugged her, and Khloe slid into my chair.

"I *know* this is something I could get used to," Khloe said, smiling and letting out a deep sigh.

Whitney and I laughed. "I haven't even chosen colors for you," Whitney said. "Show me your dress."

"Bye!" Khloe and I said as Whitney left. With a smile, the makeup artist closed our door behind her.

I'd watched every second when Whitney had applied Khlo's makeup. My BFF looked *très belle*, with makeup shades that complemented her tan. Light gold eye shadow, tinted moisturizer, a shimmery bronzer, mascara, and rosy lip gloss made Khloe look like a model.

"I wanted Whitney to stay forever," I said.

Khloe pulled off her headband. "Me too. She was the coolest, and we got *this*!"

Khloe held up a royal-purple business card with gold lettering.

I took the card, almost not sure it was real. This card was like gold. Whitney had connections in the fashion business and in entertainment. She had told us to contact her if we ever needed anything that related to her field—from potential celeb interviews and audition dates for Khloe, to fashion show tickets for me. Whitney said she couldn't make any promises, but Khloe and I were in agreement that it was more than enough to have contact with Whitney.

"The best part is that Whitney's going to e-mail us some EBTs," I said.

Khloe checked her reflection again, then turned to me. "I know! We're going to have *professional* makeup tips. Not that we didn't look killer before."

Smiling, I reached over and hugged Khloe.

"Thank you, thank you," I said as she squeezed me back. "That was the coolest present. I know you put a lot of thought into it."

"You're *very* welcome, LT. I'm so glad it worked out and that we got a makeup artist that didn't make us look twenty-five or something."

We giggled as we both reached for our dresses and laid them on our beds.

"Plus, Whitney was a present for me, too."

I stepped back so I could look Khloe in the eye. "You're making it seem as if it wasn't a big deal, but what you did for me was more than getting my makeup done. I feel . . . *pretty*. I feel confident going to my party—my first at Canterwood. That's because of you. It's a big deal."

Khloe's eyelids sparkled with gold flecks as she blinked. Fast.

"Lauren Towers!" Khloe waved her hands in front of her eyes. "I *don't* do emotional unless it's for a role or something. If you make me cry, *you* are calling Whitney and getting her back here!"

This soft side of Khloe was usually hidden beneath her upbeat, always-on personality. It made me feel more bonded to Khlo when I got to see this side of her.

I pointed to the clock. "I won't say another word. We have zero time to get Whitney back because we have to do our hair, get dressed, and be out the door soon."

Khloe looked at the time. "Omigod! We really do have to get going." She dashed to her desk, plugging in both of our large-barreled curling irons. She turned around, a gentle look on her face.

"Thank you for what you said. And I know exactly what you mean."

With that said, we turned on an upbeat mix on my iPod and got ready to party.

26

IT'S ALMOST TIME

"WE HAVE TO BE OUT OF HAWTHORNE IN ten!" I said. I was touching up my pinky nail with pearly pink polish—I'd smudged it a moment ago.

"I'll be ready," Khloe said. She was adding a few extra curls to her hair. "You?"

"Same."

I realized I was breathing fast even though I was sitting on my bed. I'd finished getting ready moments ago and was playing with my delicate, thin hoop earrings. After Whitney had left, it was as if Khloe and I had gone from zero to sixty in seconds. Accessories had been traded. Hair advice had been given. Shoes had been given a thumbs-up. Now, with time to think, I'd never felt this many emotions at once.

Nerves.

This was my first Canterwood party. On top of that, it was *my* party. What if no one but my closest friends came? What if Drew didn't show? I envisioned unlikely but possible scenarios: spilling punch on my dress, tripping and landing on my butt, dancing and looking like a crazy person.

Excitement.

I was *thirteen*. This was my party at Canterwood, and I had been waiting all month for this night. It wasn't just my birthday, it was also Halloween. That holiday would have been enough on its own to make me this giddy.

Sadness.

Becca, Ana, and Brielle weren't here. Becca and I had trick-or-treated together as long as I could remember. Even when Becca had gotten too old to snag free candy, she'd taken me and we'd felt cool and grown-up being outside after dark without Mom or Dad. Ana and Brielle loved Halloween too, and we'd even made costumes for our horses. There would be an absence of my two best Union friends, no matter how many Canterwood students came tonight. A flash of Taylor's face went through my brain. He counted among my list of friends. I wished he could celebrate with me.

Thankful.

I was still a new student at Canterwood. I'd been lucky enough to be paired with an amazing roommate. Plus, I'd found wonderful friends and, without them, getting through Canterwood would be tough, okay, nearly impossible.

I slipped back to reality when Khloe twirled in her black dress in front of me, grinning.

"Time for the reveal of the masks!" she said. "They're the last thing we need, and then it's off to the ballroom."

We each pulled boxes—mine black and Khloe's white—from our closets. I'd stayed up almost all night the day our dresses had arrived in the mail to look for the perfect mask. It hadn't been easy, and I'd combed site after website until I'd found it.

"You first," I said.

Khloe bowed her head. "Your wish, birthday girl. Here it . . . is!" She lifted the top of the box and pulled out a stunning white mask on a matching stick. The mask was shiny satin, and on the side, a quarter-size rhinestone sparkled. A giant ostrich plume, about the length of my forearm, wasn't to be missed. From the jewel, about a dozen smaller, quill-like feathers fanned out into a half circle.

"Khlo! Omigosh! That is so insanely gorgeous! It's going to stand out so well with your dress."

Khloe held the mask up to her face. "Yay! I'm so glad you like it. I thought I'd go for a really colorful one, but there was something about this mask that made me get it."

"It's perfect," I said. "So elegant."

"Your turn!" Khloe said, putting her mask down.

I unwrapped tissue paper from my mask and held it up. "Here's mine!"

"Lauren!" Khloe said. "Wooow."

I smiled, looking at my mask. It was different holding it up against my dress when Khloe was out of the room to make sure it matched than actually wearing my dress with it.

I'd chosen a Venetian-style mask that was silver with rose-colored pink around the eyes and tiny pink rhinestone swirls. The edge of the mask had a braided silver trim. In the center of the mask, a larger pink oval-shaped jewel rested on top of the mask, and dozens of thin, wispy pink feathers bloomed behind it. The stick was braided silver, just like the trim.

"That is so, so beautiful, and I don't know how you found such a great match for your dress," Khloe said.

I grinned. "It took forever. But it was totally worth it!"

We both held our masks to our faces, giggling. "Shall we?" Khloe asked, handing me my silver clutch and holding on to her black one.

"We shall."

27

THIS IS HOW CANTERWOOD PARTIES

I STEPPED INTO THE BALLROOM, LOWERING my mask. I couldn't believe I was still on campus. This looked *nothing* like the ballroom. It looked . . . like the perfect place for a masquerade party!

"Khloe!" I said. "Oh my God."

The entire wooden floor was covered in rolling fog. "I borrowed the fog machine from the theater department," Khloe said with a smile.

All of the tables were draped in satin fabric—silver, plum purple, and black. Real pumpkins with votive candles added a touch of Halloween orange to every table. And that was just what I could see from here. Pop music streamed from a sound system I couldn't see, and at least a dozen people were already here.

Feathers of all colors fanned around faces. Lighting caught jewels, glitter, and rhinestone-covered masks.

"I can't tell who *anyone* is," I said to Khloe.

"You're here!"

I turned and two girls lowered their masks. Clare and Lexa had chosen the dresses that Khloe and I had thought they'd like.

"You both look amazing," I said, with Khloe nodding in agreement.

Clare had found a purple mask to match her dress, and it was draped with black beads. "Thanks!"

Lexa had accented her tangerine-colored dress with a black shimmery mask dotted with pearls. Thin black wires curved into the air from one side of the mask, adorned with black jewels.

"Hey, hey!" Jill said, walking up to us.

Her glasses were gone, and she looked elegant in the coral lace tiered dress. Jill raised her mask to her face—it was bloodred with a fabric gold rose on the side and a matching gold stick.

"Jill, that mask is *beyond*!" Khloe said.

Jill beamed. "Why, thank you! I love yours, too. Lauren, you found the perfect mask for your dress."

"Actually, you know what's perfect?" I asked the group.

They shook their heads.

"You guys and what you did for me," I said. "This is beyond any birthday party I could have imagined. It's so luxurious and glam, I almost feel like I'm crashing!"

All of the girls smiled.

"Really," I said. "I don't know how to thank you enough."

Lexa looked at the other girls, then at me. "I think we can all agree that the only way to thank us is to start partying and have a good time!"

"Done!" I said.

We raised our masks to our faces and walked across the floor. I scanned each guy as I looked for Drew. It was practically impossible to tell them apart—some of the guys had masks that covered their heads.

I'd imagined what tonight might look like, but my imagination hadn't come close to this. The ballroom grew busier by the second. The masks gave off shocks of color—baby blue to royal blue, violet to plum, petal pink to hot pink, sunshine yellow, tangerine, clover green. Not one mask was the same, and each had a different style and coverage of the face.

A girl in a bright-blue mask with gold designs had been put in charge of the drink table.

"What can I get you?" she asked.

"I'd love a glass of Perrier," I said.

Blue Mask Girl poured my bubbly water into a clear plastic cup, handing it to me with a smile.

I thanked her and waited while the rest of my friends got their drinks.

"Happy birthday, Lauren," a guy's voice said.

I turned, and he was dressed in all black, including a black mask that revealed little of his face.

"I'm sorry!" I said. "Your mask is so good—I don't know who's under there."

The guy laughed and lifted it off.

"Garret!" I smiled at him. He was one of Zack's friends. "I'm really glad you're here."

"How could I miss this?" He swept an arm in the direction of the ballroom. "It's your birthday, and you've got a killer party."

"You should thank my friends for the party," I said. "They deserve all the credit."

"Want to dance?" Garret asked. He saw me hesitate. "Just one. I know who you're looking for."

I smiled, glad that he got it. "Let's dance!"

After dancing with Garret, my friends found me, and we danced until our feet were sore.

"Did any of you see Drew yet?" I asked.

"He's coming, Laur," Khlo said. "We haven't been here that long. Who knows—he may even already be here and waiting for the right moment to approach you, sweep you off your feet, and dip you backward into a kiss."

The rest of us giggled. Khloe *had* watched one too many soap operas, but it made me love her that much more.

"I'll wait to see if the dip and kiss happens," I said. "But I've got to find him first."

Lexa grabbed my hand, pulling me toward her. "No way! C'mon! You're not spending your entire party waiting for anyone. Let's get a group together and play a game."

"Okay, let's do it," I said.

Soon we'd found Zack, Garret, and a couple of people from our classes. I sat next to Jill on the couch and reached for a strawberry on the table.

"The best party game E-V-E-R is obvi One Pass," Khloe said. "As the official Party Planner to the Stars—in this case, Lauren Towers—I think she should go first."

Everyone started clapping.

"Laaaureen! Laaaureen!" Zack and Garret chanted.

"Totally game," I said. "Khloe Kinsella, ask away."

Grinning, Khloe sat on the arm of the couch across

from me, smoothing her dress. "Anyone not know the rules?" she asked.

"I'm a little hazy on them," said Raquel, a girl from my fashion class.

Khloe nodded. "No big. Rules are simple: One person gets to ask another three questions. The person being asked has to answer every question, *truthfully*, unless he or she says 'pass.' If, say, I'm being questioned and I don't want to answer the second question, I can say 'pass,' and then I *have* to answer the rest of the questions. Hence the 'one pass.'"

"Got it," Raquel said, tossing her long black hair over her shoulder.

"Let's play."

I locked eyes with Khloe. "Go for it, KK."

"First question. Lauren, do you have a crush on any teachers at Canterwood?"

"Ooh!" the girls chorused.

The guys all turned their heads toward me.

I blushed, glad the lighting was soft in this part of the ballroom.

"Time's ticking, Towers!" Khloe said.

"Argh! Okay!" I took a deep breath. "He's not a *teacher* exactly, but I kind of maybe think Doug's cute."

"Omigod!" all of the girls chorused.

I hid my face, holding my mask even closer, while everyone said "Ooh" and Garret and Zack made kissing sounds.

"Second question!" I said. "Anytime now!"

"Okay," Khloe said. "Have you ever been mad at your sisters and done something to get revenge?"

"Can't wait to hear the answer to this," said Lacey. She was in fashion class with Raquel, Cole, and me.

Before I could answer, a guy walked up to us. He wore black pants and a black button-down shirt, and his mask made my eyes fly open. The gold mask glittered, even in the dim lights, and tiny gold beads draped in loops around the mask. The gold stick was wrapped to the top in gold jewels, and a single white ostrich feather pulled the entire look together.

"I'm so late, but can I join the game?" he asked. His voice was deep—one I didn't recognize.

"Only if you take off that gorge mask and let us see who you are," Lexa said.

The mask lowered and a grinning Cole stared at us.

"Cole!" I said, jumping off the couch to hug him. "You totally fooled me! You got me with the different voice."

"I'm glad my attempt to be mysterious worked," Cole said in his normal tone.

"Come play One Pass," I said, taking his arm and pulling him over to the couch.

The game resumed.

"You have to answer or pass, LT," Khloe said. "What's it going to be?"

I thought about what I'd done to Charlotte years ago. Like an immature kid, I'd filled her shampoo bottle with hot-pink hair dye. She'd emerged from the shower with streaky pink hair and had cried until we'd gotten it fixed. I'd confessed, and Mom had grounded me for a month.

"Pass," I said.

Surprise showed on Khloe's face. I didn't want to recount any of the things I'd done to my sisters and embarrass them by bringing it up. I wanted the DVD to be the first step toward a better relationship among all of us. If I wanted that, truly wanted it, I couldn't answer Khloe's question.

"Okay, we have a pass! Laur has to answer the last question now, no matter what," Khloe said.

I shifted on the couch seat, nervous about what she was going to ask.

"Do you have a crush on anyone our age besides Drew?" Khloe asked.

That one was easy.

"Nope," I said, smiling.

"You're done," Khloe said, standing and motioning for me to sit in her spot. "Now you ask someone else the questions."

"Jill," I said.

28

BIRTHDAY WISH
COME TRUE

WE PLAYED ONE PASS UNTIL EVERYONE HAD gotten a turn. My mind had stayed focused on the game, most of the time, but I couldn't stop myself from looking around for Drew. Maybe he didn't come over during the game because he wanted to say hi privately.

Students were coming in and out after going on a haunted trail ride that Lexa had planned. I headed back to the drink table, when someone tapped my arm.

I turned and *knew*. No mask needed to come off. The white mask, which formed a helmet over the top of his head, also covered half of his face. Very *Phantom of the Opera*–like.

"Hi," I said. "I'm so glad you're here!"

Without a word, Drew offered me his arm and I took

it. I loved that he wasn't talking—it was as if I was on the arm of a mystery guy. It fit the theme of the night. Weaving around people dancing and feathers swaying in the air, we stepped out of the ballroom. The once-loud music turned to a quiet hum.

The Halloween air couldn't have been a better temperature—chilly, but not cold. Stars twinkled in the sky, and blackness surrounded us. The only lights came from inside, escaping through the windows, and the lanterns along the sidewalks on campus. A black horse was hitched to a small dark wooden carriage. Tiny twinkle lights had been wrapped around the front, back, and sides of the carriage. It looked like something out of a fairy tale. In the front seat, a masked man waited for us to climb inside. Drew motioned toward the carriage and I nodded.

The closer we got, the faster my heart pounded. There was *no* way Drew and I wouldn't kiss after the ride! Lexa said she'd strung lights along a path in the woods and had hung glowing paper lanterns every so often. It sounded *très* romantic!

Drew led me to the carriage and stopped. He turned to me, taking both of my hands. I held his, hoping my palms weren't sweaty.

Oh.

Mon.

Dieu.

This was it! It was happening *right now*! Before I had time to worry about my breath or if my lips were soft enough, Drew leaned in and I closed my eyes. Our lips touched softly, for a few seconds, and we pulled back. Electricity coursed through my body, like I'd touched a hot wire fence. Dazed, I stood there, staring at him. I grinned, unable to hide even a bit of my happiness.

The kiss had been everything I wanted. Actually, it had been more. I'd thought about this moment a million times, and none of my daydreams about kissing Drew had been this *wonderful*. I didn't know if I'd ever stop feeling like I was floating.

Even in the dimly lit yard, I could see his smile. I smiled back, rubbing my lips together. They tingled, and I knew it had been real.

I'd kissed Drew. I'd *kissed* Drew.

"That's the birthday present that I wanted the most," I said. "You officially made my night perfect."

He touched my cheek. "Wishing you happy birthday in person was so much better than over the phone."

Wait. What? The voice was all wrong. What happ—

The guy reached both hands to his face and pulled off his mask. A shock of cropped blond hair emerged.

I gasped, taking a step backward.

"Surprise," Taylor said, smiling. "Happy Halloween *and* number thirteen!"

ABOUT THE AUTHOR

Twenty-four-year-old Jessica Burkhart (a.k.a. Jess Ashley) writes from Brooklyn, New York. She's obsessed with sparkly things, lip gloss, and TV. She loves hanging with her bestie, watching too much TV, and shopping for all things Hello Kitty. Learn more about Jess at www.JessicaBurkhart.com. Find everything Canterwood Crest at www.CanterwoodCrest.com.

New girls.
Same academy.
And some serious drama.

Join the team at the Canterwood Crest Academy at

CanterwoodCrest.com

Only the best class schedule, ever!

- ❧ Watch the latest book trailers
- ❧ Take a quiz! Which Canterwood Crest girl are you?
- ❧ Download an avatar of your fave character
- ❧ Check out the author's vlogs (video blogs)!

Illustration © Glass Slipper Webdesign

Real life. Real you.

Don't miss

any of these

terrific

Aladdin M!X

books.

EBOOK EDITIONS ALSO AVAILABLE | KIDS.SimonandSchuster.com

Sometimes a girl just needs a good book.

Lauren Barnholdt understands.

www.laurenbarnholdt.com

From Aladdin M!X   Published by Simon & Schuster

MEET BRITTANY, CASSIE, AND ISABEL. THREE GIRLS WITH BIG DREAMS AND BIG AMBITIONS.

Sometimes the drama during the commercials is better than what happens during the show. And sometimes the drama making the commercial is even better. . . .

Did you **LOVE** this book?

Want to get access to great books for **FREE?**

Join

Simon & Schuster IN THE **bookloop**

where you can

✦ Read great books for FREE! ✦

• Get exclusive excerpts •

§ Chat with your friends §

◉ Vote on polls ◉

Log on to ◉ everloop.com

and join the book loop group!